THE GOLDEN VALKYRIE

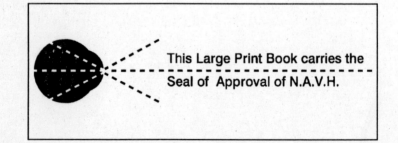

This Large Print Book carries the
Seal of Approval of N.A.V.H.

THE GOLDEN VALKYRIE

IRIS JOHANSEN

THORNDIKE PRESS

A part of Gale, Cengage Learning

GALE
CENGAGE Learning·

Detroit • New York • San Francisco • New Haven, Conn • Waterville, Maine • London

GALE
CENGAGE Learning

Copyright © 1983 by Iris Johansen.
Thorndike Press, a part of Gale, Cengage Learning.

LIBRARY OF CONGRESS CATALOGING-IN-PUBLICATION DATA

Johansen, Iris.
  The golden valkyrie / by Iris Johansen.
    p. cm. — (Thorndike Press large print famous authors)
  ISBN-13: 978-1-4104-2979-7 (hardcover)
  ISBN-10: 1-4104-2979-2 (hardcover)
  1. Women detectives—Fiction. 2. Large type books. I. Title.
  PS3560.O275G66 2011
  8137'.54—dc22   2010052334

Published in 2011 by arrangement with Bantam Books, a division of Random House, Inc.

Printed in Mexico
2 3 4 5 6 7 15 14 13 12 11

THE GOLDEN VALKYRIE

ONE

"Raphael will be waiting for you in the alley behind the hotel," Nancy Rodriguez said briskly as she deftly maneuvered the Toyota through Houston's heavy early-evening traffic. "If the coast is clear, he'll take you right up to the suite and let you in with a passkey." She grimaced. "If not, you're on your own, Honey."

"Fine," Honey Winston said absently, anchoring a strand of white-gold hair firmly back away from her face with a hairpin.

"Fine!" Nancy exclaimed, shooting her a glance of intense exasperation. "*Caramba!* You're crazy, do you know that? If they catch you, the least they'll do is take away your license. They might even throw you in jail." She tapped the folded newspaper lying between them on the seat. "The mayor is really rolling out the red carpet for Prince Rubinoff and his cousin. He's not going to be at all pleased if you provoke any unpleasant publicity."

A frown creased Honey's brow. "Even royalty has no right to behave as unscrupulously and heartlessly as he has," Honey said indignantly. "That poor woman was almost beside herself."

"That 'poor' woman is heiress to a coffee plantation the approximate size of Ecuador," Nancy said dryly. "And if you ask me, Señora Gomez appeared just a little *too* upset."

"How can you say that?" Honey asked with a frown. "She was crying as if her heart were breaking."

"And you melted, as usual." Nancy sighed, her dark eyes affectionate. "Didn't anyone ever tell you that private detectives are supposed to be hard-boiled?"

"My secretary is at me constantly about that very thing." Honey grinned teasingly, her blue eyes twinkling. "But how can I believe her, when she's such a marshmallow herself?"

"Marshmallow!" Nancy squeaked. "Me?"

"You," Honey affirmed. "You wouldn't even take a salary if I didn't practically force it on you."

"I get along," Nancy said crossly. "Which is better than you do. When I was over at your apartment last week, there wasn't anything in the cupboard but peanut butter. No wonder you've lost weight lately."

"Peanut butter is very nourishing," Honey said defensively. "All the nutritionists say so."

"Not as a sole diet, darn it," Nancy argued. "Do you know how it makes me feel to take money from you, when I know that you barely have enough to survive? Why can't you be sensible?"

"We agreed that the week I couldn't afford to pay your salary was the week you'd look for another job," Honey said, a stubborn set to her chin. "It's bad enough being poor as a church mouse. I won't accept charity."

"It wouldn't be charity, blast it," Nancy argued. "I'd be a fool if I didn't realize by now how independent you are. It would be a loan." She made a face. "Knowing you, you'll probably even insist on paying me interest."

"We've gone through all this before," Honey said gently, her eyes warmly affectionate. "The answer is still no."

Madre de Dios! Nancy exclaimed in exasperation.

Watching her, Honey hid a smile of amusement. If Nancy's hands had not gripped the steering wheel, she would have thrown them in the air with her usual Latin expressiveness. "Why do you have to be so damned dedicated and idealistic? It wouldn't hurt you to accept a little help. Why do you have to be a private investigator anyway? With your looks you could be anything you wanted. Why the hell can't you want what normal women want?"

Honey's lips twitched. "And what do 'normal' women want?" she asked solemnly, her eyes dancing.

Nancy cast her a glance of extreme irritation. "Fame, riches, and multiple O's," she pronounced impressively, then looked greatly insulted when Honey burst into giggles. "It's not funny." Then her own lips curved in a reluctant grin. "Well, maybe it is to a little Puritan like you."

"Wrong on both counts," Honey protested, still chuckling. "No one in her right mind would call me little, and I'm not a Puritan, merely discriminating."

"A virgin at twenty-four is not a Puritan?" Nancy lifted her eyebrows skeptically. "You've got to be kidding."

"Why did I let you ply me with those margaritas and encourage me to tell you my life story?" Honey asked gloomily. "You've been throwing that up to me ever since."

"If I remember correctly, you needed all

the comfort you could get that night," Nancy said dryly. "How was I to know you were practically a teetotaler? You forgot to mention that when you were mooning about the injustice of a system that allowed the sexual harassment of dedicated young sleuths like one Honey Winston."

"I guess I *was* pretty maudlin that night," Honey confessed sheepishly. Even now, thinking back on that day, she felt a twinge of anger. "I simply couldn't believe that a reputable investigator like Ben Lackland would fire me just because I wouldn't go to bed with him."

"That's because you're green as grass, Little Nell," Nancy said cynically. She shook her head wonderingly. "It constantly amazes me how a girl who was first in her class at the Police Academy and spent two years on the force could still be so blasted naive. Everyone in Houston knows Ben Lackland is a chaser as well as a king-sized rat, but you thought he was being fatherly toward you!"

"But he had such a sweet wife," Honey protested. "And he never actually tried anything until that last night in the office."

"They all have very sweet wives," Nancy said, her tone ironic. "It's an excellent insurance policy. Remind me to tell you about my ex-husband sometime. He was a great one for insurance."

"He was also crazy as a loon to ever let you get away." Honey spoke fiercely. "Some men don't know their luck."

Nancy gave her an impish grin. "Don't worry. I've made sure that every man since knows what a prize I am." She made a left turn into Fannin and then a right into the alley that ran alongside the towering white hotel that was their destination. She brought the Toyota to a halt a little distance from a wide double door, obviously used for deliveries. She flicked off the headlights and then reached up to turn on the dome light.

"Honey," she said, her face suddenly serious, "forget about this. You don't need the money badly enough to take a risk like this. There will be other jobs."

"I haven't noticed anyone beating down our door," Honey said dryly.

"It's only been six months since you opened your own agency," Nancy said persuasively. "Give them a chance. You're good, really good. The only reason Lackland didn't try anything before was that you were the best agent he had. You'd be there now if his ego weren't bigger than that pea brain of his."

"And we'd both be eating better," Honey

replied ruefully. She shook her head. "You know that we need this job, no matter what the risks, Nancy. I won't even be able to pay the rent next month without this fee." She tried to smile reassuringly, despite her own apprehensions regarding this night's task. "It's not all that dangerous. It will probably be only thirty minutes' work once I'm in Prince Rubinoff's suite. All I have to do is to locate Señora Gomez's letters and be on my way." Her lips curled scornfully. "A man like that probably keeps them under his pillow, so he can bring them out and gloat over them."

Nancy chuckled. "I doubt that. With as many women as 'Lusty Lance' is reputed to have — and have had — that could prove a trifle inconvenient." She picked up the newspaper and looked at the picture critically. "Heavens, he's a handsome stud. Just look at that face. Adonis . . . with a little touch of the devil."

"More than a little, according to the gossip columns," Honey said caustically, glancing at the picture.

Grudgingly, she had to admit that Nancy was right. That face, with its strong, regular features and beautifully shaped mouth, was arrestingly attractive, and the mischievous grin and dancing eyes saved it from being too handsome. "I'm sure that Señora Gomez would agree with them."

Nevertheless, she reached over and took the paper from Nancy, fascinated in spite of herself by that compelling face. Not that she was alone in that fascination, she assured herself quickly. Prince Anton Sergei Lancelot Rubinoff exerted a powerful charisma that was acknowledged worldwide. The younger son of the royal house of the Balkan state of Tamrovia, he had been a godsend to the media since he was a college student at Oxford. They had dubbed him 'Lusty Lance,' and that nickname had not only pertained to his formidable bedroom activities. Lance Rubinoff also had a boundless lust for adventure and life itself. In his early thirties, he had been in more scrapes than Honey could remember.

It was rumored that their Majesties were less than approving of their errant son, as was the Crown Prince Stefan. That they exerted little control over his activities was principally due to the partiality of his Uncle Nicholas, another black sheep, who unexpectedly had had the surprising good sense to marry the only daughter of Sheik Karim Ben Raschid. Young Lance had spent much of his childhood with his uncle in Sedikhan, and the sheik, ruler of a staggeringly oil-rich sheikdom, had developed a fondness for young Lance. He had deeded him a few choice acres on his twenty-first birthday, which produced enough oil yearly to buy Tamrovia outright. The cousin mentioned accompanying Rubinoff on his visit to Houston must be Nicholas's son, Alex Ben Raschid, Honey thought idly.

"Can it be that Lusty Lance is stirring a little fire under that cool facade?" Nancy asked archly, her eyes on Honey's absorbed face.

Honey quickly closed the paper and dropped it back on the seat. "Nonsense," she said briskly. "I was checking to see what time the party the mayor's giving him begins. It's at nine, and they'll undoubtedly be dining with the mayor before the party." She checked her watch. "It's eight-ten now. It should be safe to go up to the suite. You're sure that this Raphael can be trusted?"

Nancy nodded. "He's a friend of my younger brother's. The only thing you have to worry about is Raphael's luring you into a vacant hotel suite and trying to make a pass. He's got a thing for big, beautiful blondes."

Honey made a face. "Haven't most men?" she asked wryly. "I've been fighting that particular problem since I left the orphanage when I was sixteen. They all think just because I look like some damn fertility goddess that my sole role in life is destined to be flat on my back in bed, preferably their bed."

"I should be so lucky," Nancy said teasingly, gazing enviously at Honey as she opened the door and got out of the car. "I'd almost give up sex to look like you." Her brown eyes twinkled. "Of course, if I gave up sex, I wouldn't need to look like you."

In a black leotard and sheer lycra tights, Honey Winston did resemble the fertility goddess she'd derided so scornfully. Standing five feet nine in her stockinged feet, she was built along voluptuous, queenly lines, with full, high breasts, a slim waist, and long, shapely legs that most women would have given their false eyelashes to possess. Even her face had a certain sensual earthiness, owing to the passionate curve of her lower lip and the slightly slanted deep violet eyes that gave her a curiously smoldering look. Her hair was a shimmering white-gold, and she tried to detract from its rather spectacular effect by wearing its luxurious length swathed severely about her head. She'd tried cutting it once, but she'd found that when it was short, it persisted in curling riotously about her head and only augmented that provocative sensuality.

"I hadn't noticed that you're having any problem attracting admirers," Honey retorted.

"I'm not bad," Nancy admitted with a wink. In her late twenties, Nancy Rodriguez was attractive rather than pretty, with the smooth olive skin and big, dark, flashing eyes that revealed her Mexican heritage. Her medium-length brown hair was permed into a riot of gypsy curls, and was very becoming to her piquant features. "Are you sure you don't want me to wait for you?" she asked.

Honey shook her head. "After I get the letters, I'll grab a taxi back to the apartment." She smiled soothingly. "I'll call you as soon as I get home."

"You'd better," Nancy said grimly. "Or I just may come knocking on Prince Rubinoff's door." She pulled a face. "Though I'd probably have to take a number."

Honey chuckled. "Kama Sutra twenty-two?" she asked teasingly.

"Something like that," Nancy agreed absently, her expression suddenly very sober. "Be careful, Honey."

"Always," Honey said lightly. She slammed the car door and waved reassuringly before turning and walking

17

briskly toward the wide double doors.

The portable dining table moved smoothly over the plush hunter-green carpet of the hall, despite the added weight of the passenger occupying the bottom storage shelf. Why couldn't she have been one of those petite five-foot-nothing types? Honey wondered gloomily, trying to keep her long legs curled under the sheltering confines of the over-hanging white damask tablecloth.

"Okay?" Raphael called down to her cheerfully. "We're almost there, Miss Winston. It's just down the next corridor."

"I'm fine," Honey lied, knowing she'd scarcely be able to walk when she was able finally to uncurl from this pretzel-like position and get off this blasted shelf. There wasn't any use complaining to Raphael. He had done the best he could under the circumstances.

When she had met the young Latin bell-hop inside the delivery doors forty minutes ago, she had been deluged by bad news. Security for the hotel's famous guests had been tightened unexpectedly, with the locks changed on the VIP suite, and only the security officers had been given passkeys. In addition, Prince Rubinoff had canceled his plans to dine with the mayor this evening, and he and his cousin were having dinner in their suite before leaving for River Oaks to attend the party.

Honey had scarcely had time for the disappointment to sink in when Raphael had come up with an alternate plan. He had persuaded the usual waiter from the dining room to let him substitute, and he was going to smuggle Honey into the suite on the shelf under the dining table. She could hide there while Prince Rubinoff and Alex Ben Raschid dined. Once they'd left the suite, she would be able to slip off the trolley and go about her business. He had clearly thought his solution a stroke of pure genius, and Honey had fallen in with the plan out of sheer desperation. It might not be foolproof, but it was the only plan in town.

The trolley had halted now, and she heard Raphael knock softly on the door. Then there was a murmur of voices and the table was once more in motion. This time the carpet was even plusher, and of a rich russet shade, she noticed before the trolley once more came to a halt. There was a murmur of voices once again. Raphael's and two others', and then the soft closing of a door.

She was on her own. Now all she had to do was to keep absolutely still for perhaps another forty-five minutes and she would be home free. It might not be all that easy, she thought ruefully. She was already getting a cramp in her left thigh. Why didn't they sit down and eat their dinner, damn it?

The gentlemen were obviously not willing to oblige her, for she heard the soft clink of crystal across the room. Marvelous. They were going to have a cozy predinner drink. They must have carried their drinks across the room, for though their footsteps were silent on the thick carpet, their voices were suddenly clearly audible.

"You know that his honor the mayor isn't going to be pleased about this, Lance," a deep voice drawled casually. "He's not a man who's used to being stood up."

"Too damn bad." He was answered coolly. "I've put up with this bureaucratic folderol for three days now, Alex. You told me this was going to be a vacation."

"Be patient," Ben Raschid urged lazily. "A few more social duties and we'll be free to play a little. It doesn't hurt to strengthen diplomatic ties with a city as rich in technology as Houston."

"I should have known that you'd squeeze a few business shenanigans into this trip." Rubinoff's voice had an underlying note of amusement, despite its exasperation. "If I recall, you persuaded me to come with you on the pretext that it would be your last spree before you took over control of the business from your grandfather. Yet here you are, wheeling and dealing. I might just as well have stayed in Zurich."

It was odd how much you noticed about voices when you couldn't see the people involved, Honey mused. Both men were speaking in English, which wasn't unusual, considering that they'd attended Oxford together. But neither had the upper-class, public-school accent that she would have expected. Ben Raschid had a trace of a British accent, but Lance Rubinoff sounded almost aggressively American.

"You were getting bored with painting all that snow anyway," Ben Raschid replied. There was the abrasive sound of a match being struck, a short pause, and then Ben Raschid continued, "You said yourself that you were ready for a change."

Oh, my Lord, she hadn't considered the possibility that one of the men might smoke! Oh, please, let Ben Raschid be sitting far away from the table, or let it just be a cigarette. She was violently allergic to cigar smoke, and its effect on her soon escalated from violent sneezing fits to actual nausea.

"You caught me in a weak moment,"

Rubinoff said lightly. "I was finding that red-haired Olympic figure skater a trifle boring. She kept nagging me."

"Nagging?" Ben Raschid asked, puzzled. "The woman appeared to be completely crazy about you. She couldn't keep her hands off you."

Oh, Lord, it *was* cigar smoke, and Ben Raschid must be practically right next to her. Honey could feel that first tingle in her nostrils that was the ominous harbinger of things to come.

"Oh, I couldn't fault her eagerness," Rubinoff was saying gloomily. "It was her kinkiness that was the problem. She wanted to do it on the ice."

There was a short silence, and then Ben Raschid asked carefully, "It?"

Rubinoff tersely supplied an obscene Anglo-Saxon noun that caused Honey's eyes to widen in shock.

Ben Raschid exploded in laughter. "My Lord, you do know how to pick them. Nude?"

Rubinoff was chuckling now too. "Of course. She seemed to think it would be the ultimate experience," he said ruefully. "I must be getting old. Ten years ago I would probably have done it."

"Ten *weeks* ago you probably would have

done it," Ben Raschid corrected dryly. "She must have caught you in an unusually sedate mood."

The tickle in her nose was getting almost unbearable. Why couldn't Ben Raschid be a pipe smoker? Hadn't anyone ever told him that Middle Eastern potentates were supposed to be addicted to the hookah?

"Perhaps," Rubinoff admitted. "I might have been more amenable if she'd settled for an indoor rink, but she was continually raving about the magnificence of nature in the raw. It's below freezing in Switzerland at this time of year!"

It was coming. Why did this have to happen? Why couldn't everything have gone as smoothly as she'd planned? It just wasn't fair, damn it!

"I can see how you could have found that a bit dampening to your enthusiasm," Ben Rachid said solemnly. "Perhaps you could have worn —"

He broke off abruptly as Honey sneezed explosively. The sneeze was followed by two more of equal violence. They couldn't have helped but hear, Honey thought morosely. That sudden silence in the room was very expressive. Bracing herself for the coming confrontation, she waited resignedly.

The damask tablecloth was abruptly

flipped back, and she was suddenly practically nose to nose with that face Nancy had rightly described as full of the devil. The bright blue eyes so close to her own were certainly dancing with satanic mischief at the moment. His gaze traveled leisurely over her contorted figure before returning to her face.

"Are you supposed to be the hors d'oeuvres or do we save you for dessert?" Rubinoff asked politely, squatting down so that they were on the same level.

Honey gazed at him hopefully. "Would you believe that I'm a quality-control agent for the hotel, checking on the dining service?"

He cocked his head consideringly. "No, I don't think I'd believe that," he said slowly.

"I didn't think you would," Honey said gloomily. "I guess you might as well help me out of here."

"Delighted," the prince said solemnly, offering his hand and helping her solicitously from her metal nest. As she unwound to her full five feet nine, he pursed his lips in a soundless whistle of appreciation. "I underestimated you. You're not a dessert; you're a blooming smorgasbord."

But she was in no mood for clever metaphors. No wonder the smoke had affected her so quickly, she thought crossly. Ben Raschid was lounging lazily on the couch not six feet from the elegantly appointed dinner trolley, and he still had the slender brown cigarette in his hand that had been her downfall. Despite its thinness, it must have been exceptionally strong, for now that she was no longer protected by the filter of the tablecloth, it was overpowering. Her stomach lurched, and she experienced a dizzying nausea. She was going to be sick. "Oh, no," she moaned miserably, and turned and flew toward the silk-curtained window at the end of the room.

"My God, she's going to jump!" Rubinoff cried, startled, as she tore the beige drapes aside and worked frantically at the window. "You little fool, we're twenty stories up!"

Honey had the window up now and was leaning out, breathing in the brisk, invigorating coolness, when she felt two strong arms forcefully grab her from behind.

"Are you crazy?" Rubinoff asked angrily. "You could have been killed. What the hell is wrong with you?"

The fresh air was blessedly relieving her of that horrible queasiness, but she took a few more deep breaths before she risked an answer. "I wasn't trying to jump," she gasped, "I just felt sick and needed some air."

"I see," Lance Rubinoff said slowly, his arms tightening around her. "You weren't thinking about escaping, then?"

She shook her head, still breathing deeply.

He moved closer, his hands sliding up and around her rib cage to just below her breasts. "You're not even a little suicidal?" he asked softly.

"Of course not," Honey said. "You can let me go now."

"Perhaps that wouldn't be a very good idea," he said silkily, his hands moving up a fraction so that he was lightly cupping the fullness of her breasts. "You said that you were ill. What if you got dizzy and fell out the window?"

"I'm not dizzy anymore," she told him breathlessly. That wasn't quite true. She was feeling oddly light-headed, and those strong, gentle hands seemed to burn through the cotton of her leotard.

"You're sure?" Rubinoff murmured wistfully. "We wouldn't want an international incident, you know. Can't you see the headlines? Lascivious prince throws beautiful trespasser out the window."

She giggled helplessly. The man was

completely mad. "I'm quite sure," she said firmly.

"Pity," he said, and his arms dropped reluctantly away from her. He stepped back, and she turned to face him. His blue eyes were twinkling. "No one in his right mind would believe that I'd toss a luscious thing like you away under any circumstance." He raised an eyebrow mockingly. "If you get so violently claustrophobic, don't you think you could have tried to meet me some other way than hiding under that little cart?"

"I'm not claustrophobic," she said indignantly. "It was the smoke. I'm allergic to it." She pointed accusingly to Ben Raschid, who was regarding them both with quizzical amusement. "Tell him to put out the cigar."

"Put out your cigar, Alex," Rubinoff ordered obediently, his lips twitching.

"Certainly," Ben Raschid said politely, leaning forward to crush out the cigar in the crystal ashtray on the coffee table. "Anything else?"

Rubinoff turned to Honey. "Anything else?" he asked gravely.

Honey shook her head.

"That will be all, Alex," Rubinoff said grandly. "We'll let you know if she changes her mind."

"Good," Ben Raschid drawled. "Now,

bring her over here and let's get a better look at her."

Rubinoff gestured mockingly. "Milady?" Taking her by the elbow he propelled her gently across the room until she stood before Ben Raschid. Then he strolled over to half lean, half sit on the arm of the couch beside his cousin.

Honey felt rather like a slave on an auction block as they appraised her admiringly and intimately from her ballet-slippered feet to the top of her white-gold head. In sheer self-defense she stared back just as blatantly.

Both men were tanned, dressed in dark evening clothes, and were well over six feet, and there the similarities ended. Cousins they were, but they bore practically no resemblance to each other. Prince Rubinoff's dark-auburn hair and brilliant blue eyes shone like restless burning flames in contrast to the raven-dark hair and piercing black eyes of Alex Ben Raschid. Though the contrast in coloring was extraordinary, it was their expressions that truly set them apart.

Lance Rubinoff's countenance was so boldly, joyously alive that Honey found herself gazing at him in helpless fascination despite herself. It was as if he were lit from within by that flame to which she had mentally compared him. Ben Raschid's expression, on the other hand, was guarded and faintly cynical, and if there was passion behind that dark, saturnine face, it would be released only at Ben Raschid's will.

"Very nice," Ben Raschid said casually, leaning back on the couch, his gaze narrowing on Honey's lower anatomy speculatively. "Gorgeous legs. I'll flip you for her."

"No way!" Rubinoff said softly, his eyes not leaving Honey. "This one's mine. She's got me hot as a firecracker just looking at her. I think you'll have to make my excuses to the mayor. I plan on being very busy this evening."

Honey frowned fiercely. "If you're through gloating over me as if I were a piece of prime sirloin —"

"Very prime, indeed," Rubinoff murmured outrageously, and as she glared at him indignantly, he said solemnly, "Sorry. Please continue. You were saying?"

"I was about to ask what you intend to do with me," she asked tautly.

"But I've just been telling you, love," Rubinoff protested gently. "Such ingenuity deserves a reward. I'm going to skip the party and we're going to spend the evening in bed." He grinned mischievously. "Perhaps tomorrow, too." He shook his head admiringly. "God, you're a clever little puss. Cleopatra could have taken lessons from you."

"Cleopatra?" Honey asked.

"She had herself wrapped in a carpet and smuggled into Caesar's audience chamber," he explained patiently. "I'm sure she did the best she could with the materials at hand. I doubt that they had portable dining trolleys in ancient Egypt."

"From what I hear, she did exceptionally well with what she had 'on hand,' " Ben Raschid commented, his lips quirking. "A girl after your own persuasion, Miss . . ." He trailed off inquiringly.

"Honey Winston," she supplied.

The men exchanged amused glances.

"An actress?" Rubinoff asked.

"No," Honey answered crossly. She had always hated her name with a passion. "It's my real name. I was told that my mother thought my hair looked like honey when I was born."

"It must have lightened considerably since then," Rubinoff said softly. "It looks like snow in the moonlight now. How long is it when you take it down?"

"Almost to the middle of my back," she answered automatically, gazing hypnotically into those soft, glowing eyes. Then she shook her head as if to clear it. "What earthly difference does it make how long my hair is?" she demanded, almost stamping her foot in exasperation.

"I like long hair," he explained with utmost reasonableness. "It's virtually a fetish with me."

"I'm sure a man of your experience has quite a few of those," she said crossly. "I'm surprised you didn't give in to your little figure-skater's demands."

He looked momentarily surprised. "That's right! You did overhear that, didn't you?" He smiled so warmly that it took her breath away. "Did the idea appeal to you? I wouldn't mind doing it with you, sweetheart. I don't think I'd even notice the cold."

Honey mentally counted to ten before she said quite slowly, enunciating every word precisely, "No, it does not appeal to me. I do not want to make love with you on the ice, or in a bed, or on top of Mount Everest. I do not want to make love with you at all. Is that clear?"

"I didn't offer Mount Everest," Rubinoff said, his lips curving in an impish grin. "But it's not a bad idea. The thin air could make it quite an erotic experience. Perhaps we'd better think about that." He turned to Ben Raschid and asked interestedly, "You do a lot of mountain climbing, Alex. Is this a good time of the year for scaling Mount Everest?"

Ben Raschid cocked his head thoughtfully. "I shouldn't think so," he said lazily. "I'd wait a month or so, until the weather is less uncertain."

"Why don't you listen to me?" Honey wailed. "I didn't come here to go to bed with you. I came to get Señora Gomez's letters." She ran her hand frustratedly through her carefully coiffed hair, scattering pins in all directions. "If you hadn't been such an egotistical monster and insisted on keeping them, none of this would have happened."

"Letters?" Ben Raschid asked, raising an eyebrow quizzically. "Have you started collecting mementos, Lance?"

"Of course not," Rubinoff said, still gazing at Honey with that molten, glowing warmth. She wished he wouldn't do that. It had a very peculiar effect on her. "Manuela Gomez? I don't even recall receiving any letters from Manuela. Are you a friend of hers, sweetheart?"

"She hired me to get back the letters," Honey said. She was a bit relieved that at least they were beginning to listen to her. "I'm a private investigator." She glared at Rubinoff accusingly. "She was very upset.

32

She said she'd begged you to return her letters but you just laughed at her."

"A private investigator?" Lance Rubinoff asked softly. He shook his head firmly. "That's not a job for a lovely thing like you. You could get into all kinds of trouble, smuggling yourself into strange men's hotel suites."

His eyes traveled admiringly over her curves and long, shapely legs in the black tights. "I thought private detectives all wore trenchcoats and deerstalker hats. I must admit that I much prefer your outfit, sweetheart. Is it your usual garb or do you save it for burgling hotel suites?"

"Of course it's not my usual outfit," she said in exasperation. "I didn't know what I'd find when I arrived here. I thought I might possibly have to get in by way of an air-conditioning vent or something."

Rubinoff cocked his head consideringly as his eyes went to the twelve-inch-square opening of the vent across the room. His eyes returned to linger on the voluptuous swell of her breasts. "You'd never have made it, love," he said solemnly.

"I know that now," she said. "Will you or will you not give me those letters to return to Señora Gomez?"

"I don't have the slightest idea what

you're talking about," Rubinoff said, as he lazily rose to his feet. "But I have every intention of finding out. I'll just give Manuela a call and see what she's up to." He took a step closer to Honey. "We might as well take the rest of those pins out; it's falling down anyway," he added softly, his gaze holding hers. She was scarcely aware of his deft hands plucking at the remaining pins, until her hair tumbled into a heavy white-gold glory about her shoulders.

"God, that's fantastic," he breathed hoarsely. "Isn't that beautiful, Alex?"

"Beautiful," Alex agreed lightly, but his voice served to break the spell Rubinoff seemed to weave about her so effortlessly.

She took a deep breath and stepped back. "I am not a *thing*," she said firmly. "I'm an intelligent professional, not some pretty little sex object for your amusement."

"And spirit, too," Rubinoff said. "Damn, she's a sweet little th — woman," he corrected smoothly. He turned and strode swiftly toward a door on the far side of the room. "I'll call Manuela on the bedroom extension," he continued briskly. "Don't let our guest leave before I get back, Alex." He turned at the door, his blue eyes twinkling. "And don't let her put her hair back up!"

Little? She'd never felt little or lacking in

strength in her whole life until she'd encountered one Prince Rubinoff, she mused bewilderedly. Why did the man have such a weird effect on her?

"Is he always like that?" she asked dazedly, gazing blankly at the closed bedroom door.

"Most of the time," Ben Raschid said with a shrug. "Won't you sit down, Miss Winston? Lance may be some time. As I remember, Manuela Gomez can be voluble."

Honey crossed to the couch and dropped down on its cushioned surface, her eyes still fixed on the room into which Rubinoff had disappeared. "He's totally and certifiably insane," she said positively.

Ben Raschid shook his head, his dark eyes thoughtfully following her own. "No," he denied quietly. "He's quite brilliant, really. Don't be fooled by that flippant facade. Have you ever read Rafael Sabatini?" At Honey's questioning nod, he went on. "There's an opening line in *Scaramouche* that always makes me think of Lance." He quoted softly: " 'He was born with the gift of laughter and a sense of the world gone mad.' " His lips twisted mockingly. "You'll note the distinction. If a man believes the world is mad, how can you expect him to take it seriously?"

"It must be a trifle uncomfortable for

those around him who don't view life so lightly," Honey said, frowning disapprovingly.

"I don't think he's had any complaints so far." There was a suspicion of a twinkle in the dark eyes. "Certainly not from any of the women of his acquaintance."

That went without saying. Honey had just had a potent demonstration of that dizzying charm and overpowering virility. Yet she still felt called upon to protest acidly. "Evidently Señora Gomez is the exception to the rule."

"I suggest that we wait and see," Ben Raschid answered cynically. "I rather suspect that Manuela is playing a little game. If Lance says there were no letters, then they just don't exist. I've never known Lance to lie about anything. He has a positive passion for honesty." He grimaced wryly. "Which is why we try to keep him away from the company director's meetings."

"He's no businessman, I gather."

"No one expects him to be. His interests lie in other areas," Ben Raschid said carelessly. "When Grandfather deeded him his property, his only stipulation was that he cast his vote in the board meetings with mine. He knew he could trust Lance to keep his promise. He's completely loyal to those he cares about."

"Like Señora Gomez?" Honey asked caustically. "He doesn't appear to have been too trustworthy in her case. She was absolutely terrified when she couldn't persuade him to either destroy or return those letters. She was sure that her husband would discover that she'd had an affair with Prince Rubinoff."

Ben Raschid frowned. "That doesn't fit the picture either. Alonzo Gomez is usually very tolerant of Manuela's affairs as long as she's discreet. Why should she be in such a tizzy at this late date?"

"Since when are Prince Rubinoff's affairs ever discreet?" Honey asked dryly.

A smile lit up Ben Raschid's dark, guarded face with surprising warmth. "You have a point there," he admitted. "So I suppose we'll just have to wait and see what Manuela has to say, won't we?"

Whatever Manuela had to say seemed to take an inconceivably long time, for it was another ten minutes at least before Rubinoff came back into the room. It was clear that the conversation had not pleased him, for there was a dark frown on his face.

"The woman has the brain of a flea," he said disgustedly as he strolled over to the couch to stand before Honey. "And the ethical standards of the commandant of a concentration camp. I'm sorry, Honey."

"Sorry?" Honey asked slowly, sitting up straighter on the couch.

"It was Manuela's idea of a joke," Rubinoff explained, his expression grave. "I haven't called her since we flew into town, and she thought it would be a clever way of getting my attention." His scowl darkened. "Dear heaven, how I hate kittenish women!"

"But you weren't even supposed to be here," Honey said blankly, trying to comprehend what he was telling her.

"She was going to make an anonymous phone call at the dinner party tonight and have me summoned back to the suite." He grimaced. "She thought finding a luscious blonde in my suite who was supposedly sent by her would intrigue me. Like I said, she's not very bright. It never occurred to her that the blonde would make me forget that Manuela ever existed."

"Oh, I don't know. I think she's quite clever," Honey said slowly. At first she had been stunned and disbelieving, but now she felt a slow-burning anger that was greater than any she had known. "She was certainly clever enough to fool me. Your mistress must have been very pleased with herself. I was completely taken in."

It only increased her fury when he

shrugged and failed to deny the accusation. "I told you she was a fool," he said gruffly. "And she's not my mistress. Not anymore."

Honey jumped to her feet and faced him, her hands knotted into fists at her sides. "Do you mean that her charming little ploy didn't earn her a place back in your affections?" she asked caustically. "I'd have thought it would have amused you enormously, Your Highness. You're quite a one for pranks yourself, I understand. No wonder she thought that making a fool out of an innocent bystander would intrigue you."

There was an answering flicker of anger in Rubinoff's eyes. "I don't believe I've ever been accused of any real maliciousness in any of the mischief I've perpetrated," he said curtly. "And I'll be damned if I'll accept the responsibility for Manuela's little tricks." He drew a deep breath and said more quietly, "I said I was sorry. If you'll just calm down, we can discuss how I can make it up to you."

Honey was pacing up and down like an enraged lioness, her hair floating about her in a shimmering white-gold veil, her face taut with fury. "And what do you intend to do to recompense me, *Your Highness?*" she asked furiously. "Perhaps you could write me a check for my trouble. Isn't that the usual method of handling the hoi polloi? Write the lady a check and she'll forget she'd been humiliated and manipulated. After all, it was just a joke!"

"Don't you think you're being a bit unfair, Miss Winston?" Ben Raschid asked quietly. "Lance has already explained that this wasn't a part of his game plan."

"Game plan," Honey repeated bitterly. "Yes, that's really the right name for it. It's all a game to people like you, isn't it? You think that you can use people and then just throw them away like tissues. Well, I don't like being considered disposable. I may not be a member of your precious jet set, but I have more integrity than the whole kit and kaboodle of you, despite the fact that I have to work for my living!" She paused in her pacing to stand before Rubinoff, her breasts heaving, her cheeks flaming with bright flags of color. "You should try it sometime. It's a great character builder, a quality you're obviously lacking. Perhaps if you had something to occupy you besides bedding malicious little coffee heiresses and nympho ice skaters, you might develop a little."

"I agree," Rubinoff said solemnly, his lips twitching. "I think bedding a dedicated private detective would be much more inspiring."

Honey gritted her teeth to keep from shouting at him. Couldn't the man stay serious for two consecutive minutes? "I'm glad you're finding this amusing," she said fiercely. "But then, what else could I expect from a dilettante like you?"

She wheeled and strode swiftly across the room, toward the door, her back rigid with fury. "Good night, gentlemen. It's been an experience to remember, but not one I'd care to repeat." The door slammed sharply behind her.

"Somehow I don't think you managed to soothe her ruffled feelings," Ben Raschid said mockingly, taking a sip of his drink. "She still appears a trifle perturbed with you."

"Can you blame her?" Rubinoff asked tersely, frowning at the closed door moodily. "Damn Manuela Gomez!"

Ben Raschid finished his drink in one swallow and rose lithely to his feet. "As entertaining as I found it to see you under fire, I'm glad your gorgeous Valkyrie decided to put an end to the scene. We're going to be late for the party as it is. I suggest that we grab a quick bite and get on our way."

"You go ahead. I'm not hungry," Rubinoff told him absently, still staring at the door. "With all that shining silvery hair floating about her and those great blazing eyes, she *was* rather like a Valkyrie, wasn't she?"

Ben Raschid's gaze narrowed thoughtfully on his cousin's absorbed face. "It's natural that she should capture your imagination," he said slowly. "But may I remind you that the Valkyries were reputed to be very dangerous ladies?"

"But not boring," Rubinoff murmured. "Definitely not boring." He turned away abruptly and strode toward the telephone on the graceful Sheraton desk in the corner of the room. "Do you still have the card that fellow from the State Department gave you? What was his name?"

"Josh Davies," Ben Raschid answered. "I think I tossed it in the top desk drawer." He watched curiously as Rubinoff riffled through the drawer impatiently until he found the business card and picked up the phone. "He'll probably be at the party this evening. Why not wait and speak to him there?"

Rubinoff shook his head, his hair glowing flamelike under the overhead light. "This will only take a minute," he said crisply, "and I want him to get started on it right away."

TWO

"You know, of course, that I'm not going to let you get away without furnishing me with all the gory details," Nancy Rodriguez warned sternly the moment that Honey walked into the office the next morning.

"I told you on the phone last night." Honey shrugged and strolled over to the oval mirror on the wall that Nancy had insisted was an essential office expenditure. She smoothed a few errant strands of her hair back into its sleek coil while carefully avoiding Nancy's bright, curious eyes. "Señora Gomez turned out to be a lady rat on the same scale as Ben Lackland. I think under the circumstances we're justified in keeping the retainer."

"You're damn right we are," Nancy replied emphatically. "But that's not what I want to hear about, and you know it, Honey Winston." She sighed. "You're the only woman on the face of the earth who could be closeted with two of the sexiest men in the world for almost an hour and come out talking coolly about retainers. What was Prince Rubinoff like? Was he as handsome as his pictures? Did he make a pass at you? Talk to me!"

Somehow she didn't want to talk about that strange, exasperating meeting with Lance Rubinoff, even with Nancy. After she had cooled down a bit she'd realized that she probably owed Lance Rubinoff an apology for the insults she had hurled at him before she'd stalked out the door. He hadn't been directly responsible for his former mistress's misdeeds and had even apologized most sincerely and offered to recompense her. He had really acted with surprising generosity, when she considered that she had tried to burgle his suite. If she hadn't felt so manipulated and betrayed, she would never have been so unjust as to blame the prince for the woman's crimes. Perhaps she'd send him a note of explanation and apology before he left Houston.

She smiled ruefully at her reflection in the mirror. Lance Rubinoff would probably not even remember her name, much less the events of the last evening, in a few weeks' time. She'd skip the note.

"Do you really think it likely that he would

44

be interested in making advances to a trespasser?" Honey asked evasively.

"If the trespasser looked like you and the trespassee was Lusty Lance," Nancy answered promptly. Her lips curled in disgust. "You're not going to tell me anything, are you?"

"There's nothing to tell," Honey said lightly. She turned away from the mirror, crossed back to her secretary's desk, and perched on the corner. "I'm sure that, given the same set of circumstances, you'd have a much more interesting tale to disclose. But then, you're always telling me how dull I am," she said with an affectionate grin.

"Well, you've really outdone yourself this time," Nancy said morosely. "You're a disgrace to womanhood." She sighed resignedly. "I guess it's just as well; Rubinoff would be pretty strong stuff for a novice."

"I'm glad that you've seen fit to forgive me," Honey commented dryly as she stood up and strolled toward her office. "I don't suppose there have been any messages? Why should today be any different?"

"Oh, *madre de Dios!* I forget to tell you. There's a man waiting for you in your office. He's been here about thirty minutes."

"A client?" Honey asked hopefully, her face brightening. She could use a little good news, after that debacle last night.

"Could be," Nancy replied cheerfully. "He wouldn't confide his business to a lowly secretary like me. But he's fairly well dressed and has that solid-citizen look. His name is Josh Davies."

Honey crossed her fingers and held them up in a farewell salute before disappearing into her office. She could see immediately why Nancy referred to the man who rose politely from the visitor's chair at her entrance as a solid-citizen type. In his mid-fifties, his stocky body was clad in a dark-blue suit that was beautifully tailored, and his crisp white shirt was a discreet contrast. His gray-streaked hair was neither too long nor too short, but just right, and meticulously styled into smooth waves. Even his expression was smooth and bland, though his gray eyes were surprisingly keen.

"I'm sorry to have kept you waiting, Mr. Davies," Honey said briskly, coming forward with her hand outstretched. "How may I help you?"

Josh Davies's handshake was firm, and his glance discreetly appreciative as it traveled over her full graceful curves in the pearl-gray pants suit.

"I'm afraid that I'm guilty of being a little overeager, Miss Winston," Davies said with a rueful smile. "I wanted to be sure to catch you before you took on any other assignments today. It's extremely important that you start working for us right away."

"Us?" Honey asked, her brows arched in enquiry as she strolled behind her desk and dropped into the leather executive chair. "Please sit down, Mr. Davies. I admit to being very intrigued by your urgency."

"I'm with the Department of State, Miss Winston," Davies said in a low tone. "And I assure you that I'm not exaggerating the importance of the job that I have for you, or its extreme urgency. We want you to assume the duty of personal bodyguard to a foreign dignitary visiting in this country, whom we believe is marked for assassination." He pulled out a notebook from his pocket and flipped it open. "According to your dossier, you've twice acted in that capacity while you worked for the Houston Police Department — first, protecting a material witness while awaiting trial; second, guarding a television anchorwoman who received a death threat."

"Dossier?" Honey asked blankly. "You have a dossier on me?"

Davies closed the notebook and smiled soothingly at her. "We felt it was necessary when your name was suggested for the assignment. We had to be sure of both your personal integrity and your competence before entrusting you with Prince Rubinoff's safety."

"Prince Rubinoff?" Honey sat bolt upright in her chair, and her eyes widened in surprise. "You want me to protect Prince Rubinoff?"

"Actually, the job would involve the safety of both Prince Rubinoff and his cousin, Alex Ben Raschid, but naturally you would be Prince Rubinoff's official bodyguard," Davies said briskly. "The job would be essentially the same as the ones you've worked before. You'd live on the premises and accompany the prince everywhere he goes. If you feel the situation calls for backup, you need only phone me or one of my assistants and we'll see that you have the additional manpower."

"Wait a minute," Honey said slowly. "You're going a little too fast for me. Since when has the United States government contracted out its security assignments? What happened to the FBI or the CIA?"

Davies looked a little uncomfortable. "It seems that Prince Rubinoff won't permit the usual security arrangements. It's either you or nothing. He was quite adamant on

that point when he called me last night and
—"

"He called you last night?" Honey interrupted, her lips tightening. "I think I'm beginning to see the light." And she had actually been feeling guilty for her verbal attack on him! Her physical appeal for him had been obvious, but she hadn't thought that he'd go to these lengths to maneuver her into a vulnerable position. She felt a tiny stirring of disappointment that he'd used his position and clout to advance his pursuit of her. Somehow she'd thought better of him than that.

"I don't think you need to worry about an assassination attempt on Prince Rubinoff. After you investigate his little ploy, I believe you'll find that this threat comes straight from his imagination." She rose to her feet. "In any case, I'm not interested in this particular assignment, Mr. Davies. You'll have to find someone else to hold Prince Rubinoff's hand. I'm sure he can supply you with a lengthy list of substitutes. Good day."

"Sit down, Miss Winston." Josh Davies's voice was as courteous and well modulated as before, but there was a trace of steel in it now, which was echoed in the sharpness of his keen gray eyes. "We haven't finished our discussion, and I have no intention of

49

permitting you to refuse me. The stakes are far too high."

"This is my office, Mr. Davies," Honey said belligerently, "and I have no intention of —"

"Sit down, Miss Winston," Davies repeated, and this time the steel was sharpened into razorlike menace. "I wanted our arrangement to be an amicable one, but it seems you're going to require some 'persuasion.' You realize that your action last night in entering Prince Rubinoff's suite for purposes of theft was not only unorthodox but actually criminal?"

Honey sat down again. "He told you about that?" she asked, moistening her lips nervously.

Davies nodded. "He told me not to use it as a lever unless I was unable to obtain your services in any other way." His lips curved cynically. "It appears that he read your character very well, considering you have such a short acquaintance. You do know that a telephone call to City Hall from either myself or Prince Rubinoff would result in immediate revocation of your license?"

"Yes, I'd be a fool not to be aware of that," Honey replied faintly. "It was the risk I took." What an incredibly stupid risk it had been, to put her entire career on the line because she was tempted by a large fee and conned by a malicious little schemer.

Davies evidently agreed with her. "It was extremely foolish of you, Miss Winston," he said disapprovingly. He glanced at the notebook in his hand. "Understandable, perhaps, considering your present financial circumstances, but still very foolish. You're very fortunate that Prince Rubinoff is willing to forego pressing charges."

"Provided that I move into his suite," Honey said caustically. "I had no idea that the State Department was providing that type of service for visiting dignitaries."

Davies's expression soured. "I'm not acting as a pimp for His Highness, Miss Winston," he said tautly. "The position I've offered you is a legitimate one in every way. It's an opportunity that any of your colleagues would snap up in a minute. I might add that a good deal of prestige and publicity always accompanies the protection of royalty."

"I don't doubt that there would be publicity, but not the type that I'd relish," Honey said bitterly. She leaned forward, her expression earnestly appealing. "Look, Mr. Davies, if your department looks upon this as legitimate employment, surely you can see that it's totally unnecessary. Lance Rubinoff doesn't need protection." Her lips curved in a mocking smile. "Except perhaps from his ex-mistress. It's all just a trick, a huge practical joke at my expense. Prince Rubinoff obviously has a rather bizarre sense of humor."

Davies shook his head. "You seem to be suffering from a misapprehension, Miss Winston. Prince Rubinoff didn't come to us with a threat on his life. We went to him. I can assure you that the danger is quite real and that the informant is most reliable. Unfortunately, we haven't been able to convince either His Highness or his cousin to accept a live-in bodyguard. Consequently, we've had to limit our surveillance. Naturally, when Prince Rubinoff called and offered to let us have an agent on the premises, we jumped at it."

"Naturally," Honey echoed dazedly. This information put an entirely different slant on the situation. No wonder security had been tightened at the hotel last night. Not tight enough, however, she thought with a little shiver. She'd managed to breach that security herself with ridiculous ease. "Why would anyone want to assassinate Prince Rubinoff?" she asked wonderingly. "He's not even heir to the throne."

He shrugged. "It has nothing to do with

the politics of Tamrovia. The assassination plot also involves Alex Ben Raschid. Ben Raschid is the heir to one of the richest oil sheikdoms in the world, and Rubinoff, too, controls a sizeable portion of those oil fields. A double assassination would throw Ben Raschid's country into a turmoil and might instigate an overthrow of the old sheik."

"I see," Honey said thoughtfully. An oil-rich sheikdom in political chaos would be ideal strategically for any number of petroleum-hungry countries. "Then, why wouldn't they accept your help when you told them of the danger?"

"They're two very independent and self-willed men. They insisted that they could handle any problem that might come up themselves. Their refusal wouldn't lessen this country's responsibility if anything happened to them, however. Sheik Ben Raschid is inordinately fond of both his grandson and Prince Rubinoff. It would be sure to trigger an international furor."

"I can see how you'd want an agent actually occupying the suite," Honey said soberly. "But I still don't see why it has to be me. I'm sure it wasn't protection that Lance Rubinoff had in mind when he arranged for you to contact me."

"So am I, Miss Winston," Davies said

53

dryly. "You're a very attractive woman, and, considering His Highness's reputation, I'd be a fool if I didn't realize where his true interests rest." He hesitated for a moment before adding deliberately, "It doesn't matter."

"It matters to me," Honey said indignantly, her face flushing angrily. "I have no desire to spend the next few weeks dodging passes from one of the most disreputable playboys in the world."

"I'm afraid that's your problem, Miss Winston," Davies said coolly. "You're being hired for certain specific duties, and how you accomplish them is your own business. That also goes for any impediments you might encounter along the way. This is too important to us to allow you the option of refusing. Play along with us and we'll not only throw other choice plums in your direction, but we'll also make sure the media are aware that you're a government agent and not Rubinoff's latest mistress. I don't think we need to discuss the results of a possible refusal."

"No, I don't think we do," Honey said silkily. "Blackmail threats are so distasteful."

"Exactly." Davies allowed himself a small smile. "I assume that we're in agreement, then?"

Honey nodded. "It appears that I have little choice."

"None at all," Davies agreed blandly, rising to his feet. He slipped his notebook into his vest pocket, extracted a card, and handed it to her. "This number will reach me any time, day or night. Don't hesitate to use it at even a hint of trouble. I want you moved into Prince Rubinoff's suite by three this afternoon. I hope that will be satisfactory."

He didn't give a damn whether it was satisfactory, Honey thought cynically. Beneath that smooth, conventional facade Josh Davies was obviously one very tough gentleman. "I'll be there, Mr. Davies," Honey replied. "I'm sure you'd know about it if I weren't."

"Yes, of course," he said composedly. "Though it's remote at the moment, our surveillance is quite thorough. Good day, Miss Winston."

"Good day, Mr. Davies," Honey said, and sighed in resignation.

Honey knocked briskly on the door to the VIP suite and then waited impatiently for an answer to her summons. A frown of annoyance creased her forehead as the delay lengthened. After the elaborate rigmarole that had taken place downstairs at the reception desk, surely it wasn't too much to ask that she not be kept waiting in the hall like an overeager chambermaid. The reception clerk had taken care to phone the suite to check that she was welcome.

The door was flung open at last, and she was confronted by a grinning Lance Rubinoff, dressed only in a rich brown velvet robe that made his auburn hair burn even more brightly in contrast. "Welcome, Honey," he said mockingly, stepping aside to let her enter. "I've been waiting for you."

She stared pointedly at the bare muscular chest, with its thatch of springy russet hair, which was revealed by the loosely belted robe. "Yes, I can see that you're dressed for the occasion," she said caustically, her chin lifting scornfully. She sailed regally past him into the living room and dropped her cream shoulder bag on the elegant mocha damask couch. "I think we have a few things to clarify, Your Highness," Honey said briskly. "Under the circumstances we must maintain a businesslike attitude toward each other. I'm here for only one reason, and that's to protect you. I'm not here to amuse you or entertain you — either in bed or out of it! I hope we understand each other."

"Of course we understand each other," Rubinoff said smoothly, his lips twitching.

56

"You're going to do your best to protect me, and I'm going to do my best to get you into the sack. It's all very clear."

Honey's eyes widened in shock. Had the man no shame? He obviously felt no guilt at all for blackmailing her into this position. "You're not going to succeed," she said tersely. "You may think you're irresistible, Your Highness, but I have an odd fondness for an element of integrity in my men."

"Lance," he corrected, a frown wiping the amusement from his face. He straightened slowly and strolled toward her, his bare feet silent on the thick carpet. "I didn't want to bludgeon you into taking the job, damn it. I told Davies to try everything else first."

"But you used the whip when you had to, didn't you?" she charged scornfully, her eyes blazing. "When serfs get out of line, what other course is left to the aristocracy?"

"I used it," he admitted tightly, his blue eyes flickering. "Hell, yes, I used it." He stopped only a foot away from where she stood, and she could feel the vibrant heat emanating from his body and smell the heady scent of clean soap mixed with a tantalizing, faintly musky odor. "And I'd use it again without a qualm. Would you like to know why?"

"I already know," Honey said stormily,

trying to ignore the effect his virile closeness was having on her breathing. "You've already expressed yourself very explicitly on the subject, and with such *delicacy,* too!"

"I was joking, for heaven's sake," Rubinoff said roughly. "Does everything have to be real and earnest with you?"

"It's better than never taking anything seriously," she retorted, stung. "Am I to assume, then, that you don't want to take me to bed? That it's all been a complete misunderstanding?"

"Of course I want to go to bed with you," he said impatiently. "That's what this is all about. But I had no intention of yanking you struggling and screaming into the nearest bedroom. I was going to give you time to get used to the idea."

"How very considerate, Your Highness," Honey snapped. "And what if I have no intention of getting used to the idea? Would you still be so lenient with your humble subject?"

"If you call me that one more time . . ." Rubinoff began, talking between his teeth. Then he took a deep, steadying breath. "Look, I can see that you could be a little annoyed at the way you were forced into agreeing, but if you'd just listen ——"

"Didn't anyone ever tell you that royalty

doesn't have to make explanations?" Honey interrupted caustically, ignoring the storm signals in Rubinoff's eyes. "They just wave their scepters and we lowly plebians fall meekly to our knees."

"Meekly!" Rubinoff exclaimed, running his fingers through his hair in exasperation. "You're about as meek as a hydrogen bomb." Suddenly he stepped forward with lightning swiftness, enfolding her in his arms and bending her back in a Valentino-style embrace. Looking soulfully into her eyes he crooned tenderly, "I give up, sweetheart; you're much too clever for me. I was only waiting for you to walk through that door to pounce on you. As soon as they called up from reception, I dashed into the bedroom and threw off all my clothes so that I could ravish your senses with glimpses of my strong, virile body. If that didn't do the job, I was going to ply you with liquor and cocaine, until you were completely in my power, and then quench my insatiable hunger with your voluptuous form. Now that you've found me out, I can confess it all."

Honey was staring up at him wide-eyed, her eyes fixed in helpless fascination on the intense face so close to her own. "I beg your pardon," she said belligerently.

Rubinoff stared at her in blank disbelief, then closed his eyes and shook his head wonderingly. "Dear Lord, you're utterly incredible." He groaned softly. "You've got to be an imposter. How could a private detective be so damn naive?" He opened his eyes and looked down at her, his lips twisting in a wry smile. "I was joking again," he said patiently, as if to a slightly retarded child.

"Well, how was I to know that?" she asked defensively. "You did take an awfully long time to open the door, and when you did answer it, you weren't exactly formally dressed." Her gaze dropped down to his hair-roughened chest, which was now pressed closely to her own. Too closely, she thought breathlessly, because his warmth seemed to pierce the material that separated them and caused a hot, melting sensation in her limbs. She knew she should move away from this travesty of a torrid embrace, but for some reason she felt oddly weak and languid.

"The clerk got me out of the shower when he called to announce you," Rubinoff said resignedly. "I had to dry off and slip on a robe."

"Oh," Honey said weakly. His auburn hair did look slightly damp. "Well, you did say that the only reason you wanted me here was to try to seduce me."

"No." He shook his head firmly. "That's what you said. Naturally I want to seduce you. You turn me on more than any woman I've ever met. But that's not the only reason I wanted you here." His eyes twinkled roguishly. "The principle one, but not the only one. I wanted to make amends for Manuela's idiotic practical joke."

"By blackmailing me?" Honey asked doubtfully.

"I knew that you probably wouldn't be persuaded to come any other way," he said absently, his gaze fixed disapprovingly on her hair. "You've bundled up your hair again. Why the hell do you do that, when it's so gorgeous floating all around you like a silver cape?"

"It's more professional like this," she said, feeling ridiculously guilty at his disappointment.

She suddenly realized that she was still being held over his arm in that dramatic Valentino embrace. "Hadn't you better let me go?" she asked breathlessly.

"If you insist." He sighed as he pulled her upright, then reluctantly released her and stepped back. Tightening the belt of his robe, he asked, "Would you like a drink?"

"I'll have a ginger ale, if you have it," Honey answered as she followed him across the room to the mirrored bar. What was it about the man that kept her constantly in a state of uncertainty? she mused as she perched on a maroon-velvet-cushioned barstool and watched Rubinoff behind the bar deftly pouring her drink. When she had marched into the apartment a short time ago, she'd been determined that she was going to establish barriers even Houdini couldn't overcome. Yet here she was, accepting a drink and gazing bemusedly at Rubinoff's intent face as he concentrated on mixing his own bourbon and water. His lashes were ridiculously long for a man's, she noticed idly. Their russet color was sunstreaked gold at the tips.

Those lashes swept up swiftly as his head lifted, and he handed her a tall frosted glass. "Now," he said firmly, leaning his elbows on the bar and gazing at her with surprising gravity, "we talk."

"I believe we've been doing that for some time," Honey said dryly, taking a sip of her ginger ale. "We've just not been communicating."

His lips quirked impishly. "Oh, we've been communicating. Perhaps not verbally, but we've definitely been communicating." He held up his hand as she started to protest. "All right, I'll be as solemn and boringly sincere as even you could wish, sweetheart." He took a drink of his bourbon and water before setting his glass on the counter. "Let's enumerate the reasons why you should take the job Davies offered you, shall we?" He held up a long, graceful finger. "One, according to Davies's report, you need the money." He held up another finger. "Two, being my bodyguard would be an intelligent career move. Three . . ." A third finger joined the others. "It's your patriotic duty as an American citizen to prevent a possible international incident." He arched an eyebrow inquiringly. "Shall I go on? I've got plenty of fingers left if you're not convinced."

"I think you'd really be in a quandary by the time you reached that last digit," Honey said, her lips curving in a reluctant smile. "I think you've almost exhausted your stock of arguments now."

"I've left out two of the most important ones," he said softly as he lowered his hand and covered her own. "It'll allow me to rid myself of this damn guilt I've been feeling ever since I talked to Manuela last night."

"I don't have to ask what the last one is," Honey said dryly.

He frowned. "No, I guess you don't," he said tersely. "I've been fairly open on that score. Too damn open. I should have tried seduction." He picked up his glass and took another drink. His eyes met hers as he slowly lowered the glass. "I didn't want to seduce you, damn it," he said tautly. "You're not a woman to enjoy games. There's not much honesty in the world today, but I think you're an exception, Honey Winston. You deserve better than that." His hand tightened on hers, and his gaze was as direct as his tone. "I want you, Honey; I'm going to do everything in my power to make you want me, too. But that doesn't mean that I'm going to try to bulldoze you into anything." His lips twisted. "Sexual harassment isn't my style. I'm no Ben Lackland, Honey."

"You know about that?" Honey's eyes widened in surprise.

"Davies's dossier was fairly detailed." Rubinoff shrugged. "I can see why you'd be wary after such an experience, but I can't say that I'm flattered at being compared to him." He grimaced. "I hope that I'm a bit more subtle in my approach than that bastard."

"I'm sure you are," Honey said soothingly, amused in spite of herself at the indignation in his face. He looked very much like a cross little boy.

"My reputation may not be exactly pure as driven snow." His scowl became even darker as Honey choked on her drink at that gross understatement. "But I do not *pounce.*"

He wouldn't have to, Honey thought ruefully. That impish and almost overpowering charismatic virility would be potent enough.

"I'd let you set the pace," Rubinoff went on briskly. "I don't enjoy unwilling women."

Had he ever known any? Honey wondered. She hadn't the slightest doubt that he was supremely confident that he could overcome her resistance in short order. "And what if I remain unwilling?" she asked thoughtfully.

His smile lit the darkness of his face with heart-catching warmth. "Then I have a new experience in store," he said lightly. "I don't believe I've ever had a woman for a friend." His husky voice was coaxing, the blue eyes wistful and appealing. "Will you be my friend, Honey Winston?"

Honey felt a melting sensation in her breast that had no resemblance to the desire he had formerly inspired in her. "And if I still don't agree with your proposal?" Honey asked quietly.

He sighed resignedly. "Then I guess I'll just have to resume the blackmail tactics." His blue eyes twinkled. "For your own good, of course."

"Of course," Honey echoed, shaking her head in rueful amusement. The man was utterly impossible. She was beginning to realize that there was a layer of diamond-hard steel beneath that careless exterior. Yet she felt an odd sense of trust in the man beneath that mask. "Then I'd better give in gracefully, hadn't I?" she asked lightly.

She was rewarded by a smile so blindingly brilliant that she felt strangely dizzy. "Good girl," he said briskly, setting down his glass on the counter and coming around from behind the bar to stand before her. "I'm sure that I'll feel much safer with you in the next room." He gave her a wistful look. "Of course, I'd feel *really* secure with you in my bed." She chuckled and shook her head. "No?" He shrugged resignedly. "I didn't think so."

"I'm afraid that wouldn't be very practical in this case," Honey said lightly. "I've never heard that you were fond of *ménages à trois,* and my duties include the protection of your cousin."

"Alex?" Rubinoff looked decidedly uneasy. "Now, that might present a few problems."

66

"Problems?" Honey asked warily, her gaze narrowed on his face.

He put his hands on her slim waist and lifted her lightly off the stool. "Alex refuses to accept you as his bodyguard," he said ruefully, then continued hurriedly as she started to protest. "It's not you personally whom he objects to, you understand. He'd reject anyone hired for the same position." He turned her gently, his hand at her waist, and began to propel her across the living room, toward a door on the opposite side of the room. "He has no objection to you acting as my bodyguard, however. He thought you were quite charming."

"How very kind of him," Honey said ironically, wondering how she was supposed to guard someone when he wouldn't even acknowledge her as his protector. "I thought men in your position were accustomed to having bodyguards and security men buzzing around you. Why are you and your cousin so adamantly against it?"

"We value our privacy," Rubinoff said simply. He smiled at her grimly. "And Alex and I were brought up rather differently from what most people would expect. Remind me to tell you about it sometime."

They'd reached the bedroom door, and he opened it with a little flourish. "This is your room," he said, leaning lazily against the doorjamb. "There's an adjoining bath. I think you'll be fairly comfortable." His eyes twinkled mischievously. "I'm right next door, so if you need anything, just call."

"I'm the one who's supposed to be able to hear *you* if you need me," she said unthinkingly, and then could have bitten her tongue.

It was too much to expect him to let that pass. His face took on an expression of cherubic innocence. "Does that mean you'll come if I want you to?" he asked, gazing limpidly into her eyes. "Perhaps we'd better have them put in a connecting door. It would save considerable wear and tear on the carpet from the traffic back and forth."

"You know I meant that you were to call if you were in danger," she said sternly, trying to frown disapprovingly into that mischievous face.

"Unfortunately, I did," he said morosely. "We'll be dining at eight and then going somewhere later to dance. Since this is your territory, Alex and I will let you choose." He made a face. "Just don't make it any place where we might run into one of Alex's business chums or any political bureaucrats. He's promised me that the party last night was the final little social duty we'd have to suffer through, but I don't want to put temptation in his path."

Honey frowned. "Don't you think that it would be safer to have dinner in the suite? It will be difficult maintaining any degree of security in a crowd."

"But I can see that you're a woman who thrives on challenges," Rubinoff said lightly. "I feel completely safe in your capable hands." He turned away, and then looked over his shoulder to say, "Wear your hair down. We wouldn't want you to look too businesslike, would we? It might remind Alex that you're here to guard, not entertain, us."

He was gone before she could reply, and there was still a lingering smile on her face as she slowly closed the door and leaned against it bemusedly. Then she gave herself a little shake and straightened slowly. What was the matter with her? She was as languid and dreamy-eyed as a teenager who'd been asked to her first prom by the captain of the football team. Where was the cool insouciance that had been her shield and buckler for so long? It had taken less than an hour for Lance Rubinoff to raise in her a bewildering mixture of emotions. The physical magnetism she could recognize and understand, but what of that odd melting tenderness? He was as stimulating and intoxicating as those margaritas that Nancy had offered her as liquid comfort.

Just when she became convinced that the slightly mad, impish dilettante was the true Prince Rubinoff, he allowed her a fleeting glimpse beneath the glittering facade to the personality beneath. It was like trying to unravel the clues in a complicated and masterly crafted mystery thriller. And she'd always had a passion for mysteries. It was the primary reason she'd entered her profession. Well, this particular mystery might be more addictive and dangerous than any she had solved to date. She would have to guard her own emotions as assiduously as she would guard Rubinoff and Alex Ben Raschid.

She strode briskly toward the bathroom door Rubinoff had indicated. She had left her suitcases downstairs at the reception desk, in the last-ditch hope that she could convince Rubinoff to abandon his blackmail ploy. She would have to call down and have them sent up. But first she'd shower and wash her hair. She cast a cursory glance about the bedroom.

She supposed it could be considered as luxuriously elegant as the rest of the suite, but it was definitely not to her taste. The

cool-looking blue carpet contrasted perfectly with the rich cream taffeta spread on
the king-sized bed. The Louis XIV chair in
the corner of the room was cushioned in
the same patterned cream taffeta. It was all
very fastidious, expensive, and icily impersonal. Evidently this stiff, aloof beauty was
what the hotel management considered suit-
able for its most august guests. Personally,
she preferred a little more informality and
color in her surroundings, and she had an
idea that Lance Rubinoff did too.

As Honey entered the spacious blue-and-
white bathroom and began to strip off her
pants suit, she firmly dismissed Rubinoff
from her consciousness. He had been occupying her thoughts far too much lately.
She pulled the pins from her hair and let it
tumble down her back in wild silky profu-
sion. There was certainly no possibility of
her leaving her hair loose just because that
wild, impossible man liked it that way. No
possibility at all.

THREE

"Did I tell you how beautiful you are this evening?" Lance Rubinoff murmured in her ear as he took her black velvet wrap and seated her with graceful panache at the small table. "Your hair shines like silver against that black velvet. I'm glad you wore it down."

Honey fingered a long tress almost guiltily. "It had nothing to do with you. I just decided that there was no use antagonizing Alex unnecessarily." She touched the skirt of the simple black velvet sheath she was wearing. "And my intention was not to be beautiful, just discreet."

Rubinoff's lips quirked and one eyebrow arched mockingly as his gaze ran over her lingeringly. The dress in question may have been modest in cut, with its bateau neckline and long tight sleeves, which ended at her wrists, but on Honey's full, graceful figure it took on a tactile sensuality that was causing every man in the crowded smoky room to stare at her with distinct lasciviousness.

"Sorry, sweetheart, you didn't succeed," he drawled as he dropped into a chair next to her. "There's no way you could fade into the background no matter what you wore." His gaze ran around the room appraisingly. "This is quite an unusual place. Do you come here often?"

Honey shook her head, her own eyes following his about the room. "It's not my kind of scene," she answered. "But I thought you might find it amusing." She smiled impishly. "And you certainly won't run into the governor or the mayor here."

"No?" Rubinoff asked quizzically, and looked about him with renewed interest. "Have you brought us to a den of iniquity? It appears fairly innocuous."

The Starburst was a disco whose decor and loud, pulsating music fully lived up to its name. The only illumination in the large room was provided by the elaborate pyrotechnics beneath the clear plastic panels of the dance floor. The brilliant center ball of scarlet was constantly exploding into starlike fragments and then reforming once again into its shimmering, pulsing core. When combined with the throbbing music and intimate darkness, the atmosphere was curiously erotic.

"It's not that bad," Honey said absently. "It's just a meat market." A frown clouded her face as her gaze anxiously circled the room. "Where is Alex? I thought he was right behind us."

"He stopped in the lobby to make a phone call. Don't worry, no one's kidnapping him from beneath your eagle eye. What's a meat market?"

Honey felt the tension gripping her relax, and she leaned back in her chair with a little sigh of relief. "You haven't heard that particular bit of slang before?" she asked. "It refers to a bar or disco whose patrons are a trifle overly aggressive in their pursuit of the opposite sex."

"Very descriptive," Rubinoff said idly, watching the gyrating couples. "I gather that there are more moves on the sidelines than on the dance floor?"

"Exactly," Honey said with a grin. "I thought you'd feel right at home here." She tilted her head and gazed at him curiously. "That's the first time you've asked me to explain the meaning of any colloquialism. Your grasp of the vernacular is really exceptional. Both you and Alex sound like born and bred Americans."

"Alex and I were practically raised by a

Texas oil roughneck by the name of Clancy Donahue," Rubinoff explained with a reminiscent smile. "And his colloquialisms were often a good deal bluer than yours, sweetheart."

"Wasn't that a rather unusual choice of tutor for a royal prince and the heir-apparent to a sheikdom?" Honey asked, leaning forward, her face alight with interest.

"Not if you knew Karim Ben Raschid, Alex's grandfather," Rubinoff said dryly. "He's a wily old cutthroat with a healthy respect for American know-how and a fierce determination to keep what's his. Not an easy task, when the plum's as rich as Sedikhan. There have been border skirmishes there as long as I can remember, and the diplomatic maneuverings can be more dangerous than the battles themselves. Clancy was a mercenary, a smuggler, and God knows what else, before he turned up in one of Karim's oil fields twenty years ago. Karim turned us over to his tender mercies when Alex was twelve and I was ten, with instructions to do whatever was necessary to turn us from boys into men." His eyes were dancing. "Clancy's methods were a trifle unorthodox for princely training, but that suited Karim. He taught us everything from guerilla warfare to the art of bringing in a gusher. I went on my first full-fledged border battle when I was fourteen. Clancy certainly made things interesting."

"Didn't your own parents have anything to say about that?" Honey asked. "I would have thought that they would object to Karim's putting you in danger."

His lips curled in a cynical smile. "Tamrovia needed oil, like every other country. Karim knew just how to pull the right strings to get what he wanted, and what he wanted was a companion for Alex of equal birth and status to temper that Ben Raschid arrogance." He shrugged. "It was the wisest arrangement for everyone concerned. I was a thorn in my parents' serene, conventional lives from the moment I was born. I was always more at home in Sedikhan than Tamrovia, and Alex and I grew up as close as brothers."

"And what of Clancy Donahue? Is he still in Sedikhan?" Honey asked, her gaze on Rubinoff's face in the flickering lights, which illuminated his face, only to return it to shadow in the next instant. Had there been a touch of bitterness behind the cynicism in his expression?

"Clancy?" There was no question of the affection in his face, even in the dimness of the room. "Oh, yes, Clancy's a permanent member of Alex's household now. He generally accompanies him everywhere. He was mad as hell when Alex made him stay behind on this trip." He chuckled. "He tends to get a little overprotective and has a tendency to cramp Alex's style."

"I think he should have brought him along this time," Honey said, frowning. "If he won't accept my protection, there may come a time when he'll need all the help he can get."

"We're doing very well without him," Rubinoff said lightly. "And Alex was very receptive to you at dinner. Perhaps he'll even allow you eventually to instigate some minor security measures on his behalf."

Honey shook her head skeptically. "Charming as your cousin was to me, I don't think he's about to tolerate me in any capacity but as a dinner companion."

The evening thus far had proved to be surprisingly pleasant, and she had found herself amazingly at ease with both Rubinoff and Ben Raschid by the time they'd finished dinner. It had been a fascinating exercise just to observe the cheerful badinage between the men and attempt to detect the subtle undercurrents that ran beneath the surface of the mocking raillery. She could

77

well believe Rubinoff's claim that Alex was like a brother to him. It was all there to see once you peered beneath the masks they wore — respect, humor, tolerance, and genuine affection.

The bonds that had forged their relationship were so strong and long-standing that one would have expected Honey to feel like an outsider. Strangely, this was not the case. Rubinoff had gently drawn her into the magic circle, and Ben Raschid had followed his lead with the mocking arrogance she was beginning to associate with him. By the time they'd left the restaurant, she was on a first-name basis with both men and felt a camaraderie that she would never have believed possible a few hours before. She was vaguely conscious that Lance was deliberately dampening down that vibrant sensuality and giving her the time and breathing space he'd promised her, and the knowledge filled her with an odd breathless warmth.

"You thought Alex was charming?" Lance asked with a black scowl. "I wanted you to like him, but you weren't supposed to find him charming, damn it. I was the one who was supposed to dazzle you with my rapier wit and virile attractiveness. It's clear that I'll have to apply myself more assiduously to the project." He hitched his chair closer to her own, until his hard muscular thigh was pressed intimately against her own, and put his hand on her knee. "*Now* do I have your complete attention?"

Honey firmly removed his hand and placed it back on the table with a tolerant little pat. It was impossible to be angry with him when he was gazing at her with those wistful blue eyes that still held a glint of little-boy devilishness in their depths. "I have an idea that you've had a great deal too much attention from women in your career, Lance," she said lightly. "I wonder if you even remember their names."

"Not many of their names," he admitted frankly. "They're all a bit of a blur after a while." Then, as he saw the frown beginning to cloud her face, he covered her hand with his and said gently, "They didn't mean anything to me. How could I be expected to remember them, Honey? What I feel for you is entirely different."

She lowered her eyes to their joined hands, her lashes hiding the sudden jolt of pain at his callous remark. "I'd be something of a fool to believe that, wouldn't I?" she asked huskily. "Next month you'll probably be saying that to some other woman."

There was a flicker of anger in the blue eyes looking into hers. "I don't lie, Honey," he said curtly. "I don't know why or just how the way I feel for you is different as yet. I'm still a little confused on that score, but I do know that I've never felt anything quite like this before. When I lifted that tablecloth and found you curled up like a luscious kitten, staring up at me with those big violet eyes, it was as if someone had hit me in the stomach."

"Chemistry," Honey said firmly, still not looking at him. "What else could it be?"

"How the hell do I know?" he asked moodily. "If it was chemistry, why did it feel so right to have you with us tonight? It was as if you'd always been there across from me and always would be."

Her eyes flew up, and for a moment she forgot to breathe as she met the hot intensity of his. So she hadn't been the only one to feel that strange sense of belonging.

"Would you like me to go make another phone call?" Ben Raschid asked politely. Neither of them had seen him approach, but he was suddenly standing at their side, with an expression of amused resignation on his face and a distinctly sardonic smile on his lips.

Honey could feel the color rush to her face, and she tried to withdraw her hand from Lance's. "No, of course not," she said

80

a little hurriedly. "We were beginning to be a little concerned for you. You've been gone a long time."

Lance firmly foiled her attempts at removing her hand from his by possessively tightening his clasp. "Yes, we've missed you," he said absently, not taking his eyes from Honey's face. "Why don't you leave, so that we can miss you again?"

"Lance!" Honey exclaimed, shocked at his rudeness.

Ben Raschid only chuckled, his dark eyes twinkling as he shook his head reprovingly at Rubinoff before dropping into the chair opposite them. "Presently," he drawled. "At the moment I have the urge to sample the delights of this unique establishment Honey has seen fit to bring us to. On my trip from the foyer to the table, I was accosted by three women, two of whom offered to buy me a drink. The third wanted me to dance. Are most Houston women this aggressive, Honey?"

"Only at meat markets," Rubinoff answered for her, reluctantly looking away from Honey to glance at Alex with a wry smile. "I don't think he needs a definition of the term after his recent experience, Honey. I'm surprised you didn't accept one of the invitations, Alex. Didn't any of them look good to you?"

"There was a rather ravishing little red-head," Ben Raschid said. "But I decided to look the field over before deciding."

"A redhead." Lance shook his head rue-fully. "I should have known. Why bother to even browse, Alex? You know that you'll choose the redhead anyway." He turned to Honey and explained. "Alex has had a pas-sion for redheads since we were boys."

"It won't hurt to make her wait a bit," Alex said lazily, and he imperiously signaled a passing waiter. "She was a little overeager. What will you have to drink?"

Honey had finally managed to wrest her hand from Lance's grasp, and she unobtru-sively scooted her chair a few inches away from his. She was finding that hard muscu-lar thigh so close to her own very distract-ing. "Just ginger ale for me," she answered.

While Ben Raschid gave the orders to the waiter, Lance lifted a brow inquiringly. "Don't you ever drink anything stronger?"

She shook her head with a wry grimace. "Not since I discovered the peculiar effect it has on my tongue. It causes it to waggle excessively."

"Fascinating," he murmured. "I must remember that. A few drinks and I'll know all your secrets."

82

Suddenly, a well-manicured hand cut through the space between them and slapped down a fifty-dollar bill. They both looked up, startled, at the woman standing beside the table.

"That's for you, darlin'," the woman slurred, swaying slightly and smiling at Rubinoff with a smug alcoholic leer. "And there's more where that came from. No one can say that Joanie Jessup's not willing to pay generously for what she wants."

"I beg your pardon?" Lance said blankly. "Were you speaking to me?"

"You bet your boots," Joanie Jessup said, laying one unsteady hand on his shoulder and beaming at him. "You're the lucky man tonight, Red. I've had my eye on you since you came into the place. Damn, you're a handsome brute."

"Thank you," Lance said warily. "That's very kind of you. Now, if you'll excuse us?"

Honey had first been so taken by surprise that she could only stare open-mouthed at the boldness of the woman. Joanie Jessup was in her early fifties, on the plump side, and sported an elaborate bouffant blond coiffure. She was expensively if a trifle garishly dressed in a pink décolleté cocktail gown. She was also very obviously under the influence. Then, as Honey gazed from

Lance's stunned, wary face to the woman's drunken leer, she suddenly giggled helplessly. Lance shot her a glance of extreme displeasure.

"It's not enough?" The woman reached into her purse and drew out another fifty and slapped it down on top of the first. "I should have known you'd be expensive, you big gorgeous devil." She bent lurchingly, and nibbled seductively at his ear. "But you'll be worth it, sweetie. Redheads are always such passionate lovers."

"My premise exactly," Ben Raschid murmured, leaning back in his chair and observing his cousin's discomfort with every evidence of enjoyment.

"Very funny," Lance said caustically, trying to detach the woman's hold from about his neck and glaring at both Ben Raschid and Honey's grinning faces with profound disgust. "Miss Winston, I believe you're supposed to be my bodyguard," he said icily. "Well, guard my *body,* damn it!"

Honey hastily smothered her smile, but her eyes were still dancing as she said solemnly, "Right away, sir." She quickly got to her feet and leaned forward to whisper in Joanie Jessup's ear.

The plump blonde slowly straightened, her expression ludicrously disappointed.

"You've got to be kidding," she pleaded almost tearfully, reluctantly releasing Lance's shoulder and gazing gloomily from him to Ben Raschid and then back again.

Honey shook her head silently, her expression equally mournful.

Joanie Jessup slowly picked up the two fifty-dollar bills and stuffed them back into her evening bag. "You're sure?" she asked despondently, gazing yearningly at Rubinoff.

"Positive," Honey said firmly.

"What a God-awful waste," the woman murmured. "But, then, all the best-looking ones are." She turned and lurched uncertainly away.

"Are what?" Lance asked, his eyes narrowed suspiciously on Honey's face.

"Gay," Honey said simply. "I told her that you and Alex were lovers."

"You told her what?" Lance asked explosively, and Ben Raschid muttered a brief, explicit obscenity.

"Well, you told me to get rid of her," Honey said defensively, trying to hide the giggles that persisted in welling up despite her efforts to stifle them. "I knew that would be the quickest way. Alex's remark about passionate redheads gave me the perfect lead-in."

"Oh my Lord," Alex groaned, burying his

face in his hands. "If you don't murder her, I will, Lance."

"It's my privilege," Lance said grimly, standing up and pushing back his chair with barely restrained violence. He leaned over, grasping Honey by the wrist, and pulled her to her feet. "Come along, Honey."

"Where are we going?" Honey asked, startled, as he pulled her along behind him and crossed the room.

"I've got to expend my irritation by either shaking the living daylights out of you or channeling it into some other outlet." They had reached the dance floor, and he spun her onto the glowing, ever-changing plastic surface. "Dance with me, damn it!"

She danced with him, and it was like no dance she'd ever known. The music was loud and raucous, and the moves were as ritualistic and sensual as those in a primitive mating ceremony. The shifting colors and exploding pyrotechnics beneath their feet offered their own excitement, and Lance's face in the flaring crimson glow had a look of hungry sexuality that awoke an answering response in Honey. Then the music suddenly changed its wild tempo to a slow, mellow melody that was as sensual in its own fashion as the former wailing cacophony. Honey and Lance were both breathing hard, their emotions and senses as glowingly alive as the exhilarating adrenaline pounding through their bodies. They stood looking at each other for a moment and then, in silent agreement, they flowed together once again.

Lance wrapped his arms around her, cradling her in a close embrace, and her own arms slid almost instinctively under his suit coat and around his waist. Her head rested contentedly on his shoulder as they moved slowly around the dance floor. Honey was dreamily conscious only of the soft throbbing music and the strong beat of Lance's heart beneath her ear. His arms tightened around her, bringing her closer to the hard column of his thighs, and she felt a sudden weakening in her own limbs. How strange that the touch of warm hard sinews should make her feel so soft and weak in contrast. Strange and rather wonderful.

"Honey." Lance's voice was husky and velvet-soft in her ear.

"Hmmm?" she answered, snuggling closer to him.

"I'm definitely not gay."

"I know." Honey sighed dreamily. Nothing could be clearer than that fact at this moment. "Isn't it wonderful?"

His deep chuckle held a note of surprise.

"I think so," he said, "but I'm glad you agree." His lips brushed her temple in a caress as gentle as a summer breeze. "You know what you're doing to me, don't you?"

She nodded, her arms tightening around him possessively. She was vaguely aware that her conduct was totally inconsistent with her usual behavior. Her cool serenity and pragmatic approach to life seemed to be completely banished by the potent combination of the music, lights, and the physical magic exerted by the man holding her so closely it was as if there were one entity.

"Let's get back to the hotel," Lance said huskily, stopping in the middle of the dance floor. His arms were still holding her so close to his body as he turned and propelled her gently back toward the table that their hips brushed at every step. It was almost as if they were still dancing, Honey thought hazily. She was momentarily jolted from her state of euphoria by the realization that Alex was gone from the table.

"Where's Alex?" she asked, her eyes searching the room in sudden panic as she realized just how derelict in her duty she'd been in the last hour. She had let Lance beguile her into completely forgetting her purpose in being here tonight, and now Alex was nowhere to be seen!

"I'm getting a little annoyed with your constant preoccupation with Alex's whereabouts," Lance drawled, his lips quirking. "I assure you that Alex can take exceptionally good care of himself. It's me you should be concerned about." He draped her black velvet wrap about her shoulders and threw a few bills down on the table. "Haven't I demonstrated sufficiently just how much I need you? What if another Joanie Jessup appears on the scene lusting after my irresistible physique?"

"But we can't just leave," Honey protested as he took her elbow. "He's my responsibility, too. I have to find him."

"Honey, I told you that . . ." Lance started when his eye fell on a piece of folded paper in the center of the table. He picked up the note and perused it swiftly. An amused smile was on his lips as he looked up to say, "It's from Alex. It seems that after you cast aspersions on his masculinity he felt the need for a little active reinforcement. He's gone after the redhead. He says he'll see us back at the suite." He lifted a mocking eyebrow. "Tomorrow morning."

"But where did he go?" Honey wailed. "How can I protect him if I don't know where he is?"

"You can't," Lance said cheerfully as he

guided her swiftly through the nightclub to the front entrance. "So why don't you stop worrying about him? Alex will turn up early tomorrow morning, just as he promised. He knows that I've ordered the helicopter to take us to the Folly at ten o'clock."

"The Folly?"

Lance flagged down a passing taxi with an imperious hand, and the cab pulled to a smooth stop at the curb before them.

"Sedikhan Petroleum recently acquired an estate on a private island in the Gulf of Mexico about ninety miles off the coast of Galveston," Lance explained, opening the passenger door and helping Honey into the cab. He sank down in the vinyl seat beside her. After giving the driver the address, he continued. "It was formerly owned by an Englishman named Thomas Londale and became known as Londale's Folly."

"Why?" Honey asked curiously as Lance slid an arm about her shoulders and pulled her close to his side.

"Who knows? Perhaps because the island is located in the hurricane belt and Londale had all the buildings on the island built of stone. It probably cost him a small fortune just to import the building materials." His hand was playing idly with the silky hair tumbling about her shoulders. "Alex and I leased the property two years ago when we were here last, and found that it met our needs. It's close enough for Alex to keep in touch with his beloved power-play games, but private enough to allow him total relaxation if he wants it."

"And you?" Honey asked softly. "What does Londale's Folly offer you, Lance?"

His face became oddly guarded. "It gives me what I need too," he murmured, and before she could question the statement, his hand closed tightly in her hair and tilted her head back. He looked into her eyes, his own glowing with a warm intensity that made her feel oddly light-headed. "Do you know that I haven't even kissed you yet?"

It seemed incredible to her, too. The intimacy of the moments they'd shared tonight had bound them together with golden cords of passion. How strange to realize that they'd only touched each other in the most conventional ways.

"I can't wait any longer," Lance whispered huskily. "I sure as hell didn't want it to be in the back of a taxi, but I need you now, Honey."

Her eyes were wide and wondering as they gazed at the dark intent face slowly lowering to her own. The first touch of his lips was so light as to be almost tentative, a light, brushing caress that teased with a provocative gentleness, then wooed and persuaded, until her own lips were clinging to his in an exchange that was dizzyingly sweet.

Lance's hands framed her face with hands that were as gentle as his lips. "Lord, that was good," he said softly when their lips finally parted. "God, you're a sweet little thing." Then he was kissing her again, and it was just as magical as before.

"I'm not little," she protested dazedly, while his lips moved to the sensitive hollow of her throat.

"You're not?" he asked. "No, I suppose you're not. Somehow I think of you as being small and cuddly." His lips closed on hers again, and they were both breathing in little gasps when Lance spoke again. "You may not be little, but you're definitely cuddly," he muttered. His hands left her face to slip beneath her black velvet wrap and cup the fullness of her breasts. "You're so soft and round and cushiony."

Her chuckle was a trifle breathless. "You make me sound like Grandma's feather bed," she said faintly, and then gasped as his thumbs lightly grazed her sensitive nipples through the soft velvet.

"I'd like to use you as a bed," he murmured hoarsely. He lowered his head to rest it on her breast, while his thumbs rhythmically caressed her nipples. "I'd like to have these lovely mounds cradle me like fleecy pillows, and bury myself in the softness of your body." She could feel the warmth of his mouth through the velvet as he rubbed his face back and forth across her swelling fullness with a sensual, almost catlike contentment. "Dear heaven, I want that."

No more than she did, Honey thought feverishly. The muscles of her throat and chest were so taut that it almost hurt to breathe, and every touch of Lance's hands or lips seemed to leave a trail of molten fire in its wake. The words that he was whispering were as evocatively passionate as his gentle, stroking hands.

Then his hands were sliding around the back of her dress and deftly undoing the zipper. At first she was so lost in the hot sensual haze that it seemed perfectly natural to feel the warm eager fingers on the naked flesh of her back. Then, as her black velvet wrap was pushed impatiently away from her shoulders, she abruptly came to her senses. What were they doing?

"No," she whispered, putting her hands on her chest. "We can't, Lance. Let me go."

He looked up, his face as flushed and dazed as her own. "Let you go?" he asked, as if the idea were totally incomprehensible. "You know I can't do that." His lips covered her own in a kiss as bruisingly fierce as the others had been gentle, parting her lips to invade the moist sweetness with his tongue and explore it with an erotic skill that almost made her forget why she was protesting. "You see?" he gasped, coming up for air, his heart beating like a trip-hammer against her breast. "How the hell can we stop?"

"The driver," she said faintly, nodding to the silent, discreet figure in the front seat of the cab. She was so aroused that for a moment she was tempted to ignore their audience and melt once more into Lance's arms and forget everything.

Lance muttered a shocking obscenity, and his arms tightened possessively around her for a brief instant. Then he drew a deep, shuddering breath, and his embrace loosened fractionally. "Okay," he growled raggedly. "Just give me a minute."

It was a bit longer than that before he slowly released her and drew away a scant few inches. "Sorry," he said gruffly, while his shaking hands reluctantly zipped up the back of her dress. "I guess you noticed that you have a fairly explosive effect on me. I don't usually attempt seduction in the back seat of a taxi cab." He shook his head disbelievingly. "If you hadn't stopped me, I think I would have taken you without a second thought." He tucked her wrap securely around her shoulders once more, and pulled her into the sheltering curve of his arm. "Now, be still, and I just may withstand temptation until we get back to the hotel."

She was obediently still, her head tucked contentedly into the hollow of his shoulder while he stared impatiently out the window at the slow-moving traffic. "My God, it's just like rush hour even at this time of the night," he said disgustedly. "It will take us forever to get anywhere."

"Houston has a growth problem," Honey said dreamily, thinking how beautifully sculptured were the bones of his cheek and jaw.

He glanced down at her languid clouded eyes and bruised swollen mouth, and for a moment there was a flicker of amusement warring with the desire in his eyes. "At the moment I can sympathize, no, *empathize* perfectly," he said thickly. "Oh, what the hell!" His lips swooped down, and once again she felt his teeth and tongue working with erotic expertise. "We might as well do something while we're waiting." His hands slipped once more beneath her wrap and began to knead and tease her swollen breasts. "I wouldn't want you to cool down and change your mind, would I?"

There was no danger of that, Honey thought ruefully. Her body responded like a Stradivarius in the hands of a master violinist in the wild, heated moments that followed, and she wasn't even conscious of when the cab drew up in front of the hotel.

Lance was, however, and he drew quickly away from her as the cab came to a halt before the brightly lit front entrance. "Thank God," he said fervently, withdrawing a bill from his wallet and handing it to the grinning cab driver without even looking at it. Ignoring the driver's dazed murmur of appreciation, he opened the cab door. "Come on, let's go," he said curtly, getting out of the taxi and pulling her after him. "Another five minutes and I wouldn't have made it."

And neither would she, Honey thought with a profound feeling of relief. In those last few minutes in the cab she had begun to feel that it wouldn't have mattered if they'd had an audience as large as one at the Astrodome. She came eagerly into the possessive curve of his arm as he propelled her swiftly through the front entrance into the sleekly luxurious foyer.

"One moment, please, Your Highness!"

They both looked up in surprise, and there was a sudden brilliant flash. "That's great . . . just one more!"

Honey heard Lance mutter a violent oath, and his arm tightened protectively about her waist. He increased his pace, until they were almost running toward the bank of elevators across the foyer.

The sharp-faced photographer who had taken their picture was right on their heels. "Is Miss Winston to accompany you on your entire tour, Your Highness?" he asked with machine-gun rapidity. "Did you know each other before you arrived in Houston? What do their Majesties have to say —" He tried to follow them into the elevator, but Lance placed a hand on his chest and gave him a rough shove while punching the button for the penthouse with the other hand. The doors closed on the photographer's frowning, frustrated face.

"I should have told the cab driver to go around to the service entrance," Lance said with a scowl. "I didn't think there would be any reporters persistent enough to be haunting the lobby this late at night." His glance was suddenly concerned as he noticed Honey's pale, set face. "Are you all right?"

"I'm fine," Honey said numbly, brushing the hair from her eyes with a shaking hand.

"How did he know who I was?"

Lance shrugged. "I suppose Davies must have issued a press release. There was bound to be speculation when the news hounds snooped out the fact that you were occupying a room in our suite. It was probably the most discreet way of handling the affair." The doors of the elevator slid soundlessly open, and Honey preceded him dazedly from the cubicle and down the hall to the elegantly carved teak door of the suite.

Discreet. A discreet way of handling the affair. The words were so casually said. Well, why shouldn't they be? Lance probably hadn't noticed the double entendre that had struck her like a blow — for she *had* come within a breath of being one of Lance's "affairs." If that flashbulb had not rocked her to her senses, she would have crawled as eagerly into the prince's bed as any of his other playmates.

Lance unlocked the door and flicked on the wall switch, flooding the room with light before turning to face her. His narrowed eyes flickered warily. "Okay, let's have it," he said flatly. "What's wrong?"

"I think you know," she said huskily, not looking at him as she closed the door and moved slowly forward into the room, her gaze fixed desperately on the Corot lithograph on the wall across the room.

"The hell I do," Lance said roughly. "All I know is that in the taxi you wanted me as much as I wanted you, and now you're a million miles away from me. What happened?"

"I came to my senses," she said softly. "You're quite a man, Lance. You made me pretty dizzy for a while."

"Past tense?" he asked caustically. "I can't have a very lingering appeal. You seemed to have completely recovered your equilibrium." His voice was rough with frustration. "Look at me, damn it. That blasted picture can't hold such a degree of fascination for you."

Her gaze moved reluctantly to his taut, angry face. She felt that familiar melting sensation even now, as her gaze lingered on the strong male beauty of that face, with its cap of shining auburn, burnished by the overhead lights. A man had no right to be so beautiful, she thought desperately, wanting to close her eyes and shut out the sheer virile magnetism of him. "I just don't consider the game worth the candle, Lance," she said, steadying her voice with no little effort. "I don't want to be one of your one-night stands; nor do I want to figure in the

99

tabloids as your latest mistress." Her eyes darkened stormily. "I don't particularly relish the company I'd be in. Wasn't it only six months ago that you were squiring that extremely pricey call girl about the Riviera?"

"For God's sake, that has nothing to do with us," he said indignantly. "I told you —"

"I'm sure you tell all of us just the pretty lies that we crave to hear," Honey interrupted, her eyes flashing. She turned and stalked toward her room with regal dignity. "Well, I've heard all I want to hear tonight."

"Damn it, Honey, I don't lie," Lance grated out behind her. "I know what happened downstairs came as a shock to you, but if you were thinking clearly, you'd realize that it has nothing to do with what we feel for each other. And don't try to tell me that what we shared in that taxi was one-sided."

She turned at the door, her eyes bright with tears. "I didn't say that," she said huskily, her lips trembling slightly. "I wanted you. I'd be a terrible hypocrite not to admit it. I just can't tolerate being Prince Rubinoff's latest. I wouldn't know how to cope with it." She shrugged helplessly. "I'm just not that tough."

His expression softened, the anger dissipating. He shook his head slowly. "You're not tough at all. You're a sweet, loving woman, and I want every single bit of you." He smiled ruefully. "But I guess I can wait a little longer. Run along and hide your head in the sand, sweetheart. You'll have to surface sometime, and when you do, I'll be here waiting."

"I mean it, Lance," Honey said gravely, her face troubled. "I don't want this type of relationship. I have no use for it in my life."

"I know you mean it." Lance smiled lovingly at her, his blue eyes twinkling. "But that doesn't mean you won't change your mind. I'm told that I can be a very persuasive fellow."

The door was closing behind her when he called softly. "Honey?"

She paused.

"I'll order breakfast for nine," he said. "If you have any packing to do, do it tonight. We'll be leaving for the island promptly at ten."

FOUR

Londale's Folly proved to be a tiny tropical island set like a glittering emerald in the azure waters of the Gulf. From the air it appeared to be scarcely two miles across, with the only habitation a large stone house on the crest of the hill overlooking a sheltered cove. When the orange-and-cream helicopter was secured on the concrete landing pad in that same sheltered cove, Honey found that the notion there was only that one house on the island wasn't precisely correct.

Ben Raschid turned to Lance, one dark eyebrow arched inquiringly, as he picked up his small duffel bag from the pad. "Shall I tell Justine that you'll be up to the house for dinner?" he asked.

Lance shook his head. "Not tonight," he said absently, picking up his own small case as well as Honey's much larger one. "I have some work I want to do while the light is good. We'll rummage in the kitchen for something to snack on. Justine usually stocks the refrigerator pretty well."

His eyes flicked with sudden amusement to Ben Raschid's face. "Besides, I don't think you'd be very entertaining company this evening, Alex — you're looking a bit on the frayed side. I imagine that you'll opt for an early night. Was your redhead worth it?"

"Inventive. Very inventive," Ben Raschid replied with a distinctly Mephistophelian grin. "But she wasn't a real redhead. I'd say she was originally a Scandinavian blonde, like our Honey, here." He gave a mocking bow in Honey's direction. "Though not as beautiful, of course."

"How disappointing for you," Lance said, his lips quirking as he took Honey's arm. "I'm glad that she made up in talent what she lacked in fire."

He turned Honey and gently propelled her forward, away from the helicopter. He looked over his shoulder to say, "We'll be up at the main house for brunch tomorrow at ten. I trust you'll be recovered enough to act the proper host. I know what a churlish bastard you can be, but we wouldn't want to disillusion Honey so early in your acquaintance."

Honey heard Ben Raschid's amused

chuckle behind them, but Lance had accelerated his pace, and she hadn't time to glance behind as he hurried her from the landing pad down a gently sloping gravel path to the beach that she'd noticed from the air.

"Where are we going?" she asked breathlessly, trying to keep up with him. "And why isn't Alex going with us?" Then, when he didn't answer but continued to gaze at the horizon, she skidded to a stop and jerked her arm from his grasp. "Will you answer me, Lance?" she demanded in exasperation.

"What?" he asked absently, then apologized a trifle sheepishly. "Sorry, Honey. I was just admiring the play of the sun's rays on the water. The light is absolutely incredible here, isn't it? The only place that might possibly equal it is in Greece. There are times when Delphi appears to be bathed in liquid gold." His gaze went back to the horizon. "This island is much more arresting during a storm, though."

"That's utterly fascinating," Honey said caustically. "Now will you please tell me where you're taking me?"

Lance took her arm again. "We're almost there." He nodded to the curve in the beach ahead. "I have a small cottage on the beach, which I use when I'm here."

"You mean that you two don't even stay in the same house while you're on the island?" she asked. At his gentle nudge she once again fell into step with him, her eyes on his urbane face. "And may I ask how I'm supposed to maintain any kind of security if you're on opposite sides of the island?"

"We're not on opposite sides of the island," he said patiently. "The main house is only a five-minute walk from the cottage, and as for security, we couldn't be safer. The only permanent residents are Nate and Justine Sonders, who take care of the big house. Justine is cook and housekeeper, and her husband acts as general handyman." He darted her a mischievous glance. "They're both in their late sixties, so I think Alex and I may be able to handle them if they become *too* obstreperous."

"Very amusing," Honey said crossly. "They may be the only residents, but no island is totally inaccessible."

"This one comes pretty close. This is the only cove that's not too rocky to permit access by boat, and if a helicopter tried to land anywhere on the island, we'd hear it." He frowned at her impatiently. "Relax. We're both a hell of a lot safer than we were in Houston. Your only problem is going to be how to avoid getting a sunburn while you're playing on the beach. I hope you brought a bikini."

She shook her head. "I never wear one." She felt a sudden relief as she realized that Lance was probably right. If the island was as inaccessible as he'd said, then it would be fairly easy to keep an eye out for trespassers.

"Never?" Lance raised an eyebrow. "I don't know if I like the idea of your appearing in the altogether before anyone but me. The cove is fairly private, but it's visible from the big house. Perhaps you'd better wait until after dark to go skinny-dipping."

Honey's eyes had been searching the terrain for possible landing spots, but as the last words sank in, her eyes flew back to his face. "Skinny di—" she exclaimed. "What on earth are you talking about?" Then, as she met the dancing blue devils in Rubinoff's eyes, her own lips curved in a reluctant smile. "I meant I wear a very respectable maillot," she told him sternly. "A bikini on a woman of my proportions has a tendency to look a bit skimpy."

"An effect much to be desired," Lance murmured, his glance moving over her with a lingering intimacy that caused that hot, glowing warmth to kindle in the pit of her stomach. "All that lovely skin must be well-nigh mind-boggling. You're sure you won't go skinny-dipping with me?"

"I'm quite sure," she said firmly, frowning at him.

"Pity," he said morosely, shooting her a sly sidelong glance. "I guess we'll just have to confine it to the bathtub. Oh, well, it'll be cozier there anyway."

Honey shook her head ruefully. The man was totally incorrigible. Trying to distract him, she asked quickly, "The main house seems to be quite large. Why don't you stay there?"

He shrugged. "We both like to have our own space. It would take considerably more rooms than the Folly possesses to reconcile our two life-styles. I'd probably drive Alex up the wall in a matter of hours. My clutter would grate on that high-powered computer he calls a brain like the sound of nails on a chalkboard."

"Clutter?" Honey asked.

His expression became oddly guarded. "I paint a little," he said casually. "I'm afraid I have the usual artistic disregard for order." He made a face. "To be less euphemistic, I'm a complete slob."

"I don't remember reading anything in the papers about your being an artist,"

Honey said slowly. Actually, though, now that she thought about it, hadn't Alex mentioned something about Lance's painting when she had been crammed beneath that trolley? "Have you ever had a show?"

Rubinoff shook his head, his expression closed and tight. "I'm strictly an amateur," he said curtly. "And the gossip columns don't have access to *every* facet of my life." They had rounded the headland and come upon a white stone cottage with surprising suddenness. "Here we are, such as it is."

When Lance threw open the door and allowed her to precede him into the cottage, Honey realized what he meant. The interior seemed smaller than she had thought at first glance. Evidently the former owner had not wasted much of his extravagance on this tiny place. They entered directly into the principal living area, which consisted of a combination lounge/kitchen that was surprisingly stark and ascetic. There was no furniture at all in the room, with the exception of a black leather couch, a teak coffee table, and a scarlet leather breakfast booth in one corner of the room, opposite an ancient kerosene stove. Instead of carpet or tile, the floor consisted of polished flagstones in a dull slate blue. Two doors opened off the central area, and it was toward the farthest of these that Rubinoff headed.

"There's only one bedroom, with an adjoining bath," he said briskly as he threw open the door. "I've converted the other one into a studio. The light is better from the north." Then, as she started to protest, he waved her impatiently to silence. "Don't worry; there's a couch in the studio that I can bunk down on." He arched an eyebrow inquiringly. "That is, if you insist on being so selfish about sharing your bed."

"I insist," Honey said softly, glancing into the bedroom. It was as sparsely furnished as the other room, containing only one double bed, covered in a durable forest-green denim spread, and a strictly utilitarian night table. "I suppose the flagstone flooring is very practical in this climate," she commented. "It's probably cool no matter what the temperature."

"More practical than you'd imagine." Lance's tone was dry. "It was Londale's only sop to conventional practicality when he built the cottage. Located on an open beach, with nothing to shelter it, on an island that's smack dab in the hurricane belt?" He shook his head ruefully. "Every time the island is hit by a tropical storm, the cottage is completely flooded."

"So that's why it's furnished so meagerly," Honey said thoughtfully. "Don't you find it inconvenient to have to move to the main house whenever there's a storm?"

"It doesn't happen that often," he said casually, crossing the room to put her suitcase on the bed. "We'll probably only use the island a few months a year, and the chances of a really bad storm's hitting while we're here are minimal."

"Not if you plan on using it in September," Honey replied lightly, following him into the room and dropping her purse on the bed beside the suitcase. "Didn't anyone ever tell you that this is definitely not the season for island hopping?"

"I think I'll get to work," Lance said, and there was a barely restrained eagerness in his face that was oddly intriguing. "I'll see you later. Why don't you slip into that depressingly sensible swimsuit and go play on the beach? There should be something in the refrigerator if you get hungry later."

The door closed behind him, leaving Honey to stare at it in rueful bewilderment. So much for the trepidation she'd had about staving off Lance's amorous advances. He might just as well have told her to run along and not bother him. Not exactly uplifting to the ego. After those tempestuous moments in the taxi last night and his blunt threat before she'd left the room, she'd been distinctly wary. It appeared she'd definitely overestimated her attraction for Rubinoff.

Though both Lance and Alex had been charming to her on the trip from Houston, she didn't fool herself that either man had been pursuing her. She might almost have been a younger sister, for all the sexual awareness Alex had shown, and except for a few teasing remarks, Lance had displayed the same platonic affection.

In fact, Lance had been a little more distracted than Alex. There had been that curious leashed eagerness, a charged restlessness that had seemed to electrify him from the moment they'd met in the living room of the suite for breakfast this morning. He'd been rather endearingly like a little boy anticipating a special treat. Well, the little boy had gone off to play with his paints, and she'd been sent off to the beach with her pail and shovel to amuse herself.

She didn't ask herself why she was experiencing this weird sense of betrayal, as she turned and briskly unstrapped her suitcase. She withdrew the maligned maillot and looked at it critically. It wasn't all that stodgy, she thought defensively. Though not cut exceptionally low in the bodice, it had the popular French cut that made her legs look deliciously long and shapely, and its nude color was provocative in itself. Not that there would be anyone to provoke, with Lance locked in that room with his precious canvases.

He hadn't even made mention of her hairstyle, coiled in the usual businesslike style this morning. Not that it mattered to her, she assured herself. The less he noticed about her, the more pleased she would be. She was glad to be left alone to enjoy herself without masculine interference. She'd take a swim and explore the island and then come back to fix them a bite to eat. No, she'd fix herself a bite to eat. Lance could just shift for himself — if he decided to come out and grace her with his royal presence, she decided, and she began to unbutton her blouse. The less she saw of that impossible man, the happier it would make her.

Honey was frowning with annoyance, and her violet eyes were stormy as she traversed the last few yards to the front entrance of the Folly the next morning and knocked peremptorily on the brass-bracketed oak door. She knew that she was in no fit temper for a social breakfast, but there was no way

112

she was going to remain by herself any longer in this so-called island paradise.

The door was opened by a small, plump woman dressed in a dark dress and a pretty flowered smock.

"How do you do. You must be Justine," Honey said, forcing a polite smile. "I'm Honey Winston. I believe Alex Ben Raschid is expecting me."

The woman smiled with quiet friendliness. "Mr. Ben Raschid is breakfasting on the terrace, Miss Winston," she said. She gestured toward an arched doorway on her left. "If you'll go right through, I can get back to my kitchen."

She turned and bustled away, and Honey obediently made her way through the arch into the spacious room, which was as different as chalk and cheese from the barren cottage she'd just left. She cast a glowering look at the gleaming white terazzo floor, covered with glowingly colorful scatter rugs, and the graceful cushioned white rattan furniture as she made her way toward the French doors. The room was full of lush green plants and bouquets of flowers, and everything about it was polished and well maintained. This aspect, more than any other, served to aggravate Honey's annoyance. If there was one thing that she wasn't feeling at the moment, it was cosseted and lovingly cared for.

Her displeasure must have been mirrored in her expression, for Alex's dark brows lifted in mock surprise as he slowly got to his feet when she strode out on the flagstone terrace.

"Don't say anything," he said, motioning to a graceful white wrought-iron chair at the elegantly appointed glass table. "Just sit down and have a cup of coffee. I gather Lance has gotten himself into your bad books. I rather thought he would." He poured a cup of hot fragrant coffee from the carafe on the table into an exquisite china cup. "He's not showing up for breakfast, I gather?"

"I really wouldn't know," Honey said shortly, plopping down in the chair he'd indicated. "I haven't seen him since yesterday afternoon." She glared at him crossly. "And I have no need to cool off. I'm not in the least annoyed. I just thought that someone should have the courtesy to show up and make an explanation."

A little smile tugged at his lips, and his dark eyes glinted with amusement. "I see," he said slowly. He refilled his own cup and set the carafe back on the table before resuming his seat and leaning lazily back in his chair. "Naturally, I appreciate your courtesy as well as your charming company," he drawled with an enigmatic smile as he stretched his jean-clad legs before him. "Drink your coffee," he urged quietly. "Justine is serving strawberry crepes this morning, and you won't even know what you're eating if you don't calm down."

"I am calm," she retorted indignantly. "I'm not in the least upset." Then, as she met the cool derision in the dark eyes opposite her, she admitted reluctantly, "Well, perhaps I'm a *little* upset." She rushed on hurriedly. "But it has nothing to do with Lance. It's this blasted island. I'm a city girl. I don't know what to do with all this fresh air and glorious nature in the raw."

"And you had no wild Scaramouche to keep you entertained," Alex added softly, taking a sip of his coffee.

"I told you that he had nothing to do with it," Honey said, frowning at him fiercely. "My relationship with Prince Rubinoff is strictly business, and I certainly have no right to expect him to treat me as anything but his bodyguard." She bit her lip vexedly. "I'm just not used to not having anything to do." She looked up hopefully. "Lance said this was going to be a working holiday for you. I'm pretty good at hunting and pecking on the typewriter — perhaps I could help."

Alex shook his head immediately. "No way," he said definitely. "Lance made it very clear that you're out of bounds for me in any capacity. I've no desire to provoke that redheaded temper of his by trespassing on his property." He held up his hand as she started to protest. "I know, you're just his bodyguard." He lifted his cup and took another sip of coffee. "But we both realize that Lance is aiming for another type of relationship entirely. If I gave you something to do that would take you out of his immediate orbit, he'd raise the roof."

"He doesn't even know I'm on the same island," Honey said tartly. "He didn't come out of that studio all night, and when I knocked on the door this morning, he didn't even bother to answer." She pouted mutinously. "I don't think you need to worry about purloining my services."

"It's not unusual for Lance to get caught up in his work and labor through the night," Alex said quietly. "Particularly when he just gets back to it after an absence. Give him a day or so, and he'll surface to the point of being moderately civilized again." His lips quirked indulgently. "He's always just like a kid let out of school at first."

Honey took a drink of her coffee, not really tasting it, her gaze fixed unhappily on the delicate floral design on her cup. "I noticed," she said. "Are you as enthusiastic about your hobbies, Alex?"

"Hobby?" His dark eyes narrowed on her face. "Painting isn't a hobby with Lance; it's a full-scale passion. Didn't you see any of his work before he shut himself into his studio?"

She shook her head. "He couldn't be bothered to do anything but pat me on the head and send me off to play," she said. She looked up, a flicker of curiosity piercing the hurt. "If painting is such a passion for him, why haven't I read about it in the tabloids? He certainly makes no effort to avoid publicity. His life's an open book."

"Is it?" Alex asked mockingly. "I think you'll find when you get to know Lance a little better that he's an intensely private person concerning the things he cares about. If an item appears in the gossip column, you'll know that Lance doesn't give a damn about it. I doubt if more than five people in the world know that he's an artist." He lifted his cup in a little salute. "You should be honored, Honey."

"Is he any good?" Honey asked.

"Good?" A curious smile lifted the corners

of his lips. "Yes, I think you might say he's good. Would you like to see one of his paintings?"

"You have one here?"

"In the library," Alex said, rising to his feet. "It's a portrait of my grandfather. Lance gave it to me for my birthday last year." His dark eyes were veiled. "I believe you might find it quite interesting."

Honey's first impression as she entered the book-lined library was how small the room was. Then she realized with a sense of shock that the room was quite spacious; it was the large portrait on the wall over the desk that was dwarfing and dominating the room and producing that curious shrinking effect. Karim Ben Raschid was dressed in the traditional robes of his desert people, but that was the only conventional aspect of the portrait. His booted feet were crossed and propped insolently on a massive desk, which was as sleekly modern as he was roughly barbaric. "A wily old cutthroat," Lance had called him, and it was all there in the strong, sensual face and gleaming dark eyes that were so like Alex's own.

But there was more, too. There was determination in the set of that bearded chin and a certain tenderness in the curve of his lips. Or was it mockery? She moved forward in compulsive fascination. No, she was sure it was tenderness. She shook her head in bewilderment as she noticed a fugitive devil in the depths of those ebony eyes, which had at first not been apparent. The more she looked, the more that was revealed to her.

"Well?" Alex's voice was amused, and she could feel his eyes on her from where he leaned indolently against the doorjamb.

"Is it as good as I think it is?" Honey asked in a hushed voice, not taking her eyes from the painting. "It's the most powerful portrait I've ever seen!"

"It's great," Alex agreed quietly. "And it's not even his best work. Lance prefers not to paint anyone he has a personal attachment to. He says that it ruins his perspective."

"But why hasn't he had a show? Any gallery in the world would be proud to display paintings of this caliber." She tilted her head, trying to determine what masterly technique Lance had used to make that barbaric figure in the frame come alive.

"You'll have to ask Lance about that," Alex said. "I just thought you ought to know that Lance isn't simply a dabbler amusing himself. It may help you to accept a few of his eccentricities." There was a thread of amusement running through his voice.

119

"Like completely ignoring you for days at a time."

She reluctantly turned away from the painting, and faced him. "Thank you," she said thoughtfully. "I do understand better now."

"Good," Alex said with a grin that illuminated his dark, cynical face with surprising warmth. "Then Lance owes me one." His brow arched mockingly. "And believe me, I always collect."

She just bet he did, Honey thought, looking at that face that was as forcefully enigmatic as the one in the portrait above her. "Do you have to make excuses for your cousin very often?" she asked lightly.

He shook his head. "I don't usually bother. If Lance doesn't give a damn, why should I?" The mockery faded from his face. "But this time I think the situation's a little different."

"Different?" Honey asked.

"His reactions regarding anything concerning you have been a bit unusual, to say the least. I have an idea that he'll mind very much that he's made you upset with him."

"Not enough to interrupt his work, evidently. Not that I'd expect him to, of course," she added quickly.

"Of course not," he said solemnly, his lips

120

quirking. "As you say, it's strictly business between you two." He gestured for her to precede him from the library. "And since you're so adamant on that score, I don't feel in the least guilty about enjoying your exclusive company at breakfast. Come on along and try Justine's strawberry crepes. Perhaps you're in a better humor to enjoy them now."

The strawberry crepes were delicious, and Alex's conversation over breakfast was fascinating and carefully impersonal. He had little chance to enjoy his own breakfast, however. He was interrupted twice with business calls from Houston and once with an urgent call from Sedikhan.

When he returned to the table after the third call, he shook his head ruefully. "Sorry about that. I've told Justine to hold my calls until after breakfast."

"And this is a vacation for you?" Honey asked lightly as she sipped her coffee. "Lance said you were something of a workaholic."

"The pot calling the kettle black," he replied, refilling his cup. "He's as bad as I am. He just refuses to acknowledge that what he does is work. He calls it an enjoyable pastime and completely different from my dull, stuffy business affairs."

121

"But you don't look at it the same way, do you?" Honey asked thoughtfully, her eyes on his face.

"Very perceptive of you," he said softly, looking up. There was a flicker in the depth of his eyes. "No, I think we're both artists. I just use a different brush and a wider canvas." His eyes narrowed. "And I can assure you that the colors I select are just as carefully considered."

"But not always subdued," Honey said with an impish grin. "I noticed that you have a distinct preference for red."

"Everyone has his little quirks," he said, grimacing. "And Lance makes damn sure that everyone is conversant with mine."

"Have you always had this passion for redheads?" Honey asked lightly.

"As long as I can remember." His expression was ruminative. "I've often wondered if it had something to do with Lance."

Honey's eyes grew round. "You mean that you . . . ?"

"No, I do *not* mean that," he rapped sharply, scowling at her with extreme displeasure. "And I'd appreciate it if you'd refrain from giving out tales to that effect even in the performance of your blasted duty."

"Sorry," Honey said, trying to hide a smile.

Evidently she didn't succeed, for Alex continued to frown at her fiercely. "I should hope so," he said emphatically. Then he sighed resignedly. "What I meant was that it might have some psychological connection to my relationship with Lance," he explained patiently. "I'm a very cynical person. My grandfather made sure of that, for sheer self-protection. Lance has been the only person in my life whom I've ever trusted totally. There's a possibility that I may be attracted by women of similar coloring because I feel safer with them."

"Not because they're more passionate, as you implied?" Honey asked, her eyes twinkling.

"Well, that, too," he replied, with an answering grin. Then, as if remembering his annoyance with her, he said belligerently, "And I'd like to state categorically that I've never been attracted to a member of the same sex, redheaded or not. Is that clear?"

Honey nodded meekly. "Very clear."

"Good," he said, relaxing. "Now that we've got that settled, why don't we go back to the library, and you can choose a few books to read? They may come in handy

123

when Lance opts out of the human race again."

When Honey opened the door to the cottage two hours later, it was as silent as when she'd left. She cast a speculative glance at the closed door of the studio on the way to her bedroom but resisted the temptation to knock. Surely the man couldn't still be painting. That would be carrying his artistic marathon into the realms of the ridiculous. No, she must just assume that he wanted to be left alone, and indulge his whims. She was a mature woman, and certainly didn't need anyone to amuse her, as Alex had suggested.

She dropped the armload of books she was carrying on the bed in her room and swiftly changed into her nude-colored maillot. It was still a little damp from her swim yesterday afternoon, she noticed, and felt clammy against her skin despite the noonday warmth. She supposed she really should have brought another suit with her. This island living was going to be very hard on her meager wardrobe, and how was she going to keep her clothing clean, when there wasn't even an automatic washer in the cottage? She'd just have to go up the hill to the big house and ask Justine if she could use the one at the Folly.

The door of the studio was still stubbornly closed when she left the cottage, and she determinedly looked away from it as she passed. If he was still in there when she returned from her swim, she would have to breach his privacy even if it did annoy him. She had to be certain that he was all right, didn't she? She'd be derelict in her duty if she let a full twenty-four hours go by without setting eyes on the man. There was a satisfied smile on her face as she ran lightheartedly down to the beach.

"Don't you have any sense at all? You're going to burn to a crisp, staying out this long."

Honey felt her heart leap in her breast at the sound of the familiar voice, but she didn't open her eyes. She was much too content just lying here on the beach with only the blanket between her and the soft cushiony sand.

"I have sunscreen on," she said composedly. "I haven't been out nearly as long as I was yesterday, and I didn't get even a little sunburned then."

"It was late afternoon when you went out yesterday," he said grimly. "The sun was a good deal lower." When she didn't answer, he let out an impatient imprecation. "For heaven's sake, will you open your eyes? I feel like I'm talking to a corpse."

She reluctantly did as he asked, and then wished she hadn't. He was standing only a few feet from where she was lying, and he looked much too disturbing. The tight faded jeans he wore, hung low on his hips and molded the powerful column of his thighs with loving detail. He was shirtless, and her eyes were drawn compulsively to the beautifully sculptured muscles of his shoulders and chest. He was almost copper-colored, she noticed dreamily, and the thick russet thatch of hair on his chest was burnished by the sun to a shimmering vitality. He was unfolding a white sheet that he was carrying, and the muscles of his arms and shoulders rippled with a supple beauty as he shook out the material and dropped it over her.

"I'll smother under this," she protested, pushing the fabric aside impatiently as he dropped to his knees beside her.

"Too bad," he said coolly, drawing the sheet up to her chin again. "It's better than second-degree burns. Perhaps it's wiser that you don't wear a bikini. The more of you that's covered, the better, if you're always so criminally careless on the beach."

"Aren't you overreacting?" she asked crossly, sitting up and brushing her hair away from her face. The movement caused the sheet to fall to her waist, and she brushed his hand aside as he attempted to pull it up again. "And this suit isn't all that staid," she said huffily.

"So I noticed," he said dryly, his eyes on the lush swell of her cleavage. "When I glanced out of the studio window, I thought you'd decided to go skinny-dipping after all. It was quite a shock to my nervous system. That color is as erotic as hell."

"I wouldn't have thought you'd even notice," she snapped, and then could have bitten her tongue. She had meant to be cool and completely uncaring and not even refer to the past twenty-four hours of loneliness. She rushed on brightly, trying to mend the break. "Alex said he would send Nate down later this afternoon to see if you'd be free for dinner this evening."

He sighed gloomily, running his hand restlessly through the fiery darkness of his hair. "I really blew it, didn't I?" he asked ruefully. "I suppose it's too late to apologize. Will it help if I promise you that it won't happen again?"

"According to Alex, it isn't a promise that you're likely to keep," Honey said huskily, not looking at him. "And you certainly don't have to make me any extravagant promises. You don't owe me that courtesy; I just work for you."

"Ouch!" he said, making a face. "If that particular prevarication didn't annoy the hell out of me, it would really hurt." His blue eyes were serious as he continued quietly, "Look, you have every right to be upset, because I give you that right. I'd be bloody well furious if you went off and forgot about me for that long." He shrugged wearily. "I don't even have a reasonable excuse. I just got involved and worked through the night. I only meant to take a catnap this morning, but I guess I must have passed out." His voice was curiously grave. "Will you forgive me?"

She looked up, about to deny the necessity for the apology, when she encountered the seriousness in the blue eyes. "Yes, I forgive you," she said instead. Then, with a reluctant honesty, she admitted, "I was lonely."

"God, I'm sorry, Honey," he said, drawing a little closer to her so that they were only inches away. He reached out and took her shoulders in his hands, holding her with a careful gentleness that gave her a richly treasured feeling. "I should have realized that I'd get carried away." His lips curved ruefully. "I guess I couldn't believe that I'd fall into my usual bad habits with you only a few yards away. I sure as hell couldn't think of anything else the night before."

"But then I had no competition," she said lightly. "How could I expect to rate your attention when genius was burning and the muse whispering in your ear?"

"I'd rather have you whispering in my ear," he said with a twinkle. "And I don't lay claim to any special talent; it's just a pleasant hobby."

"Not according to Alex," Honey said slowly, gazing at him earnestly. "And not if that painting in Alex's study is an example. You're absolutely fantastic, Lance."

"Alex must have been in a very talkative mood this morning. And it's not my artistic talent that I want you to appreciate. Would you like to know what else I'm fantastic at?"

"No," she said promptly, frowning at him reprovingly. "That particular talent is a matter of public record. I'm more interested in your unpublicized talent. Why haven't you had a show? It's not fair to hide a gift like that from the world. A talent of that magnitude carries a certain responsibility."

He sighed and shook his head resignedly. "I should have known you'd fasten those gorgeous white teeth on the subject and worry it until you pried it out of me." His expression sobered. "The truth is, I can't exhibit. It would blow the whole caper."

Honey's eyes widened. "Caper?" she asked.

He nodded unhappily. "One of those art experts would be bound to recognize my technique, and neither Alex nor I have a fondness for jail cells."

"What on earth are you talking about?"

"Sedikhan Petroleum went broke two years ago," Lance said, not looking at her. "It's only the money Alex and I have been able to pour into it from our scam that's kept it from becoming public knowledge. We couldn't let old Karim lose face with his people."

"Scam?" Honey asked, subdued.

"I do the painting, and Alex takes care of passing it discreetly into the right hands to set up the miraculous discovery of another lost masterpiece. You know the Rembrandt they found buried in that cellar in Munich eighteen months ago?"

She nodded.

"That was one of mine," he said sadly. "One of my best works. I hated to let it go."

"A forgery?" Honey squeaked. "You're a forger?"

"You needn't put it so crudely," Lance said, flinching. "It takes a great deal of work

130

and a certain flair to imitate another artist's techniques. I spent more time and effort on *my* Vermeer than he ever did on his."

"Vermeer?" Honey repeated dazedly, feeling as if she were going mad.

"Woman at the Mirror," Lance supplied tersely. "Discovered last summer in Antwerp."

"Oh, my God," Honey breathed. All that incredible talent wasted on a shoddy confidence game. It made her physically ill. "That one too?"

He nodded slowly, still not looking at her, but she could see that his eyes were suspiciously bright. This confession was evidently not easy for him.

He said thoughtfully, "I suppose my greatest challenge was the Mona Lisa. The subtle shading for that one required great . . ." He glanced down at her shocked face and gaping lips and couldn't go on. He burst into great whoops of laughter, bent almost double with the force of the convulsions that shook him. "Oh, Lord, it's like taking candy from a baby," he gasped, wiping the tears from his eyes. "You're totally unbelievable, Honey. Tell me, have you ever bought the Brooklyn Bridge?"

"It was all a joke?" Honey asked blankly, and when he nodded, she felt a surge of hurt and anger of stunning strength. To think that she'd actually felt sorry for him. "You must have thought me very stupid, Your Highness."

The laughter was quickly wiped from his face and replaced by concern. "Honey," he started, "I never meant —"

"I suppose I am rather gullible," Honey interrupted, the stupid tears rushing to her eyes. "It must have been great fun for you. I should be honored to have provided you with an amusing anecdote to laugh about with Alex." She drew a quivering breath. "Do you know that I was even dumb enough to feel sorry for you? How absurd could I be to think that you could feel deeply about anything? Butterflies don't think or feel, they just flit on the surface of life and look pretty." Her voice rose bitterly. "No one expects them to be taken seriously or be anything but what they are. I just made the mistake of forgetting that. I assure you it won't happen again."

She jumped to her feet and was several yards away before he caught up with her. He grabbed her by the shoulders and whirled her to face him. "I'm not a butterfly, damn it!" he said forcefully, giving her a little shake. "I may be a blind, stupid fool not to realize that I was hurting you by my teasing, but I'm not the callous bastard you think me. I'll match my sensitivity against yours any day. What the hell is wrong with not wanting to lay your emotions out in the open for everyone to see?"

"Nothing. Not as long as you're willing to admit that they exist," she spat back. "But you're not, are you? I know very well your paintings must be important to you, but you won't admit even to Alex that it's more than an amusing pastime. Why don't you face up to the fact that what you could give the world is very special, and stop hiding it as if it were something to be ashamed of?"

His face was as taut and stormy as hers. "What do you know about it?" he asked roughly, his blue eyes blazing. "Okay! So it's important to me. Maybe it's the single most important thing in my life. Does that satisfy you?"

"No!" she shouted. "Why the hell don't you have a show?"

"Because it *is* important, damn it," he said, with equal force. "Do you think I want to be known as just another celebrity artist? My work means something. I won't have it held up as a playboy's idle dabblings."

"But the critics won't do that," Honey protested. "They couldn't. All they'd have to do is to take one look and know that you're exceptional."

"Would they?" he drawled cynically. "I think we've established that you're a bit naive. Starving artists may be taken seriously, but not princes of the blood. I don't doubt that my work would sell, but I'd never know whether it sold because someone wanted a conversation piece by Lusty Lance to hang on the wall. Well, I'll be damned if I'll give it to them. I'd rather let the canvases pile up in a deserted warehouse."

There was such passion in his face at that moment that it took her breath away — passion and a painful bitterness that caused her to ache for him. "You're wrong," she whispered huskily. "So wrong. It wouldn't be like that."

"No, you're the one who's wrong," he said tersely. "I've seen it happen often enough. Believe me, I'd find the kind of success you're wishing on me a hell of a lot more frustrating than keeping my work strictly sub rosa for the rest of my life."

"But it's such a waste," she said, and suddenly the emotions that had crowded one upon another in the past few minutes took their inevitable toll, and two tears brimmed in her eyes and rolled slowly down her cheeks. "Such a criminal waste."

There was a curiously startled look on his

face as he slowly lifted his hand to her wet cheek and gingerly traced the path of her tears. "For me?" he asked wonderingly. "I don't believe anyone's ever shed tears on my behalf before. I think I like it."

"Why would anyone cry for you?" she asked brokenly. "Have you ever shown anyone that there might be someone who was worth a few honest emotions, beneath that clown's mask you wear?"

"I've changed my mind. I don't like it," he said huskily. "Stop it, Honey. I can't stand what it's doing to me."

"Too bad," she said, the tears falling faster. "I can't say that I like it either. I don't want to cry for you. You don't deserve it."

"I know," he said, almost humbly, as he drew her into his arms and cuddled her comfortingly. He pressed his lips to her temple. "But you can't take those tears back. You gave them to me and they're mine now. I'm going to keep them in a special place somewhere near my heart, and take them out when I feel particularly wicked or sad." He was rocking her gently. "I'll look at them and say to myself, 'See, you can't be all that bad, Lance, old boy. Honey cried for you.'"

"You fool," Honey sobbed, her arms sliding around to clutch at him fiercely. "Damn, you're such a crazy fool. Why am I letting you do this to me?"

His hand was stroking her hair now. "Because every Harlequin has to have a Columbine," he said softly. "And I think I've found mine at last. God, you feel right in my arms, love."

Her face was buried in the springy russet hair of his chest, and it felt deliciously rough against the smoothness of her cheek. He smelled of clean soap and salt and a slight muskiness that was potently virile, but oddly enough, for the first time in their relationship, she was not experiencing that almost overpowering physical magnetism. She felt only a magical sense of being protected and cosseted and an almost painfully poignant tenderness.

Lance tilted her head up, and the expression on his face was oddly stern. "Honey?" he asked gravely.

She shook her head bewilderedly. She wasn't entirely sure what he was asking of her, but she had an idea that it was more than she could yield in the turbulence of the moment. "Not yet, Lance. Please, not yet."

He regarded her thoughtfully for a moment, before nodding slowly. "I can wait a little longer," he whispered, "but it's getting more difficult all the time. Remember that, will you, Honey?"

She nodded, her expression as serious as his. "I'll remember."

"Good," he said, and bent to take her lips with infinite tenderness. "Lord, you're sweet to love."

So was he, Honey thought dreamily as he reluctantly released her. Strong and beautiful and wonderfully tender.

"Come on," he said gruffly, slipping an arm about her waist and turning her firmly toward the cottage. "My willpower is eroding rapidly. My parents may have had the bad taste to throw in a Lancelot with my other more sedate names, but I can assure you that I'm no knight in shining armor."

He looked very much like one to her at the moment. Patience and restraint weren't among the qualities for which Lance was noted, making his control all the more praiseworthy.

"Well, do you want to go up to the Folly for dinner?" he asked, arching an eyebrow mockingly. "I promise that I'll be the perfect escort, to make up for my bad manners, which you've so graciously forgiven."

Honey shook her head. "No," she said quietly. "You don't really want to go." She shot him a sidelong glance, her lips curving in an amused smile. "I think you want to get back to your studio, don't you?"

He frowned. "I'm not about to do that to you again," he said curtly, but she noticed he didn't deny it. "I intend to devote the entire evening to you. If you don't want to join Alex, we'll do something else. What would you like to do?"

He spoke as if there were all the choices in the world on this tiny island.

"Well, I'm having a hard time choosing between Pavarotti's concert and Baryshnikov's *Nutcracker*," she drawled wryly. "So I think I'll settle for a good book and an early night. Alex supplied me with a surfeit of the former, and I hardly think I'll be disturbed once you get back to your work, so I'll certainly get the latter."

"I told you —" he began impatiently.

"Yes, I know," she said soothingly. "But you should have learned by now that we peasants aren't accustomed to noblesse oblige." She smiled at him gently. "I want you to work, Lance."

"You're sure?" he asked, his face troubled.

"I'm sure," she said serenely. "I'll see what I can throw together for a meal before you disappear for the evening."

He was silent for a moment. "I don't suppose you'd want to come in and keep me company?" he suggested tentatively. "The couch is fairly comfortable, and the lighting is better than anywhere else in the cottage, if you're planning to read."

Her startled gaze flew to his face. "You don't mind people around when you're working?"

His shrug was oddly awkward. "I don't know," he said simply. "I've never let anyone into my studio before. I just think that I'd like to have you there with me. It may take some getting used to for both of us." His arm tightened on her waist. "Will you come, Honey?"

Her throat was suddenly so tight, she was having trouble swallowing, and she looked hurriedly away so that he couldn't see the mistiness in her eyes. "Yes, I'll come," she said softly.

FIVE

Who could imagine that watching a man in the esthetic pursuit of painting a picture could be such a sensual experience? Honey wondered dreamily. The soft, almost inaudible whish of the brush on the canvas, the quiet sounds as Lance shifted his stance or moved to reach for another tube — even the acerbic smell of turpentine and paint was ambiguously stimulating. Honey grimaced ruefully. She must really be far gone to find the smell of turpentine an aphrodisiac. Why not be honest and admit that it was the man himself whom she found so fascinating?

Her gaze ran lingeringly over the intentness of Lance's face as his eyes narrowed in concentration on the canvas sitting on the easel in front of him. She couldn't see the painting itself from where she was curled on the cream naugahyde couch across the room, but she could see Lance very well indeed.

He was rather like a painting himself, she thought. He was wearing the same faded jeans he had this afternoon, but he had donned an old blue chambray work shirt when he had gotten back to the cottage. Its sleeves were rolled up to the elbow, baring his tanned muscular forearms, and he'd left it carelessly unbuttoned almost to the waist. Honey could see the play of the sleek muscles of his shoulders as he moved, and the light blue of the shirt turned his eyes to deep sapphire.

Suddenly those sapphire eyes darted to where she sat with her book lying ignored on her lap, and a brilliant smile lit the bronze darkness of his face. "Okay?" he asked gently. "You're not bored?"

"I'm fine. This thriller Alex lent me is really absorbing," she lied shamelessly. She hadn't read a page in the hours that she'd been in the studio this evening. She'd been too enthralled with the infinitely more exciting mystery that was embodied in the form of Lance Rubinoff. "Would you like some more coffee?"

"Not now," he said absently, his attention once more on the canvas in front of him. "You'd better use that afghan. It's getting cooler, and your legs will get cold in those shorts."

Honey's lips quirked wryly as she remembered the lascivious glance she'd received from him when she'd appeared in these white shorts earlier in the evening. At the moment she could have had fence posts for legs, for all he cared. She obediently pulled the beige-and-rose crocheted afghan over her legs and gazed contentedly around her.

The studio, though much larger than her bedroom, was even more starkly furnished. Other than the couch she was resting on, there was only a large, paint-spattered work table jammed against the wall; it was cluttered with an assortment of paint and brushes. The easel was in the center of the room. There were canvases everywhere, some leaning against the wall beneath the bank of windows overlooking the beach, and others stacked carelessly in the corners. When Lance had opened the closet door to take down the afghan from the shelf, she had even seen several other completed canvases pushed randomly against the wall in a corner. She'd been tempted to protest Lance's deliberate offhandedness with those valuable paintings, but she wasn't about to disturb the felicity between them.

She'd felt a twinge of pain even as she'd

prowled around the room gazing at the canvases he treated so carelessly. Each one was more brilliant than the last, and by the time she'd put the final canvas aside and made her way slowly to the couch, she was utterly drunk on the power and passion that leaped out of those paintings.

It was a real tragedy to keep these paintings hidden away where no one could enjoy them. There must be some way to convince Lance to exhibit his work, but at the moment she was unable to see it. She wasn't about to give up, however. For now it was enough to be here and watch the play of expressions on that strong, mobile face and let the crackling vitality that surrounded him like a visible aura flow into her. She scooted further down on the couch, resting her head on the cushion, and pulled the afghan up about her shoulders. She dropped the paperback on the floor. Lance probably wouldn't glance her way again for hours, so she needn't keep up the pretense of being interested in anything but the red-haired man across the room.

She was being carried, held in warm, strong arms, and her face was pressing against that lovely rough cushion that she recognized at once. She rubbed her cheek contentedly against him. "Lance?" she murmured sleepily.

"Shh," he whispered softly. "Go back to sleep, baby. I'm just taking you to bed. It's very late."

"Did you finish your painting?" she asked drowsily, snuggling closer to his vibrant warmth.

"Almost. I still have a bit of background to do."

She was gently deposited on a cushioned softness, and then the mattress sagged beside her as Lance sat down and calmly began to unbutton her orchid sun-top. "You shouldn't do that," she said sleepily, not opening her eyes. It was a token murmur rather than a protest. She felt it was somehow natural and fitting for Lance to be undressing her with those wonderfully gentle hands.

"You'll be more comfortable," he said, and his explanation seemed entirely logical. She heard his deep chuckle. "You needn't worry, Honey. I'm not about to try to seduce you tonight. I'm so exhausted that I can barely move." He had stripped off her top and was undoing the front clasp of her bra. "I just want to cuddle up to you and go to sleep. Okay?"

"Okay," she murmured. She could think

of nothing more desirable than those warm secure arms holding her and closing out the darkness of the night.

The rest of her clothing was stripped from her, and he was gone for a few minutes. Then he was back on the bed, drawing the denim coverlet over both of them. He pulled her close and settled her head in the curve of his shoulder, her long white-gold hair splaying in a silky curtain over his chest. His warm naked skin felt hard and rough against her own soft curves as his arms held her close with the sexless affection of a little boy with his favorite teddy bear.

"Lord, this is nice," he said, already half asleep. "Isn't it great to be together like this, sweetheart?"

She nodded with equal contentment. Her arms tightened lovingly about him and she went peacefully to sleep.

The gentle tugging at her nipple sent a tiny thrill of heat through her, and she moved restlessly, trying to hide once more behind the veil of sleep, which had been pierced by sensation. Then the tugging increased in tempo and a warm strong hand enclosed her breast and began a kneading motion that completely ripped the veil aside.

She opened her eyes to the gray predawn

hours of the morning and was unsurprised to see Lance's fiery red head at her breast. His tanned hand curled around its full whiteness appeared gypsy-dark in contrast.

"I thought you were exhausted," she said drowsily, her hand reaching down to stroke his hair.

He lifted his head with an impish grin. "I said I was tired, not dead, sweetheart. Even if I was, I'd probably have risen like Lazarus from the tomb at the sight that met my eyes when I opened them just now." His head bent, and his warm tongue gently stroked the nipple he'd already roused to button hardness. "It was dark in here when I undressed you, or I wouldn't have been able to nap even the little I did. My God, you're magnificent, love."

"Thank you," she said shyly, feeling the color mount to her cheeks.

"You're welcome," he said with equal politeness. There was a distinct twinkle in his blue eyes as he looked up again. "I love that grave-little-girl air you have sometimes. It's such a contrast to all this lush pulchritude that it blows my mind."

His hand resumed that slow, arousing kneading motion, and Honey felt a tingling in the pit of her stomach that was rapidly escalating into an aching need. "I don't think this is very wise," she said breathlessly as his teeth nibbled with erotic delicacy at the taut nipple.

"I do," he replied thickly. "I think it's the wisest thing I've done since I met you. I had to be crazy not to do it before. We both know we've been wanting it since the moment we met. Isn't that true, Honey?"

She nodded slowly. "Yes, I suppose it is," she said quietly. It was all so clear now that she'd accepted that simple truth. She had never wanted anyone in her life before this red-haired Scaramouche had appeared on her horizon, but she knew now that she must have realized even that first evening that they would eventually reach this point of no return.

He drew a long, deep breath and gave her a smile of such loving sweetness that she felt her throat tighten with emotion. "You won't regret it, love. I'll pleasure you, I promise."

"I know you will," she said tenderly. Everything that he was and did pleasured her. She knew now that he always would. "I hope I can please you, too."

"Good Lord, how could you help it?" His other hand reached up to cup her other breast. "Just looking at you is enough to make me lose control." One thumb raked the proud, hard peak that crested the voluptuous fullness of her breast, and a shiver of pure desire shot through her. His hand moved down to the softness of her belly and traced a delicate pattern on its silken smoothness. "You're like a lovely blank canvas just waiting for the first brushstroke to bring you to life." His lips moved swiftly down her midriff, dropping a trail of light kisses along the way. His teeth bit teasingly at the softness of her belly, and she inhaled sharply. "I want to paint you with the scarlet of passion." He gently parted her thighs. "I want to shade you with the gold of fulfillment." His hands were probing at the warm center of her being, and she made a sound that was half gasp at the incredible sensations that he was producing. He looked up and smiled with tender satisfaction. "And when you sleep in my arms afterward, I want you to be glowing with the dark rose of contentment." His hand moved with deft erotic expertise, shooting a jolt of hot, tingling pleasure to the heart of her. "Will you let me paint you with all the colors of loving, Honey?"

"Oh yes," she gasped. She felt as if she were already stroked with flames. "Yes, Lance, please."

He moved over her, parting her thighs and

coming swiftly between them. Leaning down, he kissed her with a hot, lingering sweetness. "I don't think I can wait any longer, sweetheart," he muttered roughly, his chest moving raggedly. "It seems I've been waiting forever for you already."

"Then don't wait any longer," she whispered, her lips parting as she drew his mouth back to hers. His tongue entered into the moist sweetness, and he made a sound in the back of his throat as her tongue responded with a wild sensuality that she'd never felt before.

His hips thrust quickly forward, and her sudden cry was lost beneath his lips. He raised his head, his body stiffening in surprise. His face was a mask of shock as he looked down at her. "Honey?" he asked dazedly.

"It doesn't matter," she muttered feverishly, her hands clutching fiercely at his shoulders. The sensation was indescribable, she felt both gloriously, tantalizingly full and achingly incomplete. "Please don't stop."

"Oh, Lord, I don't think I can," he said thickly, his hips starting a rhythmic thrusting that sent an explosive heat rocketing through her. She writhed in an agony of molten need as he lifted her hips in his hands, drawing her closer to him with each movement.

The rainbow spectrum of hues that he'd promised her was all there as he moved with her, encouraging her with words of need and praise that he gasped in her ear in a litany of passionate longing. But he hadn't told her of the incredible sunburst of sensation that would result with the fusion of those colors.

When they were lying clutching each other dazedly in the exhaustion that was the aftermath of that multi-hued storm, she tucked her head into the hollow of his shoulder. Her hand resting below his heart drawing comfort from the strong, rapid beat that was gradually slowing. "You left out quite a bit, you know," she said dreamily. "You never mentioned the deep crimson of giving and this lovely lavender-mauve weariness."

His lips brushed her temple tenderly. "I discovered quite a few new shades myself," he said huskily, his hand stroking her hair gently. "Some of them I never even dreamed existed. You're quite an artist yourself, Honey Winston." His hand paused a moment in its stroking, and his voice was oddly troubled. "You shocked the hell out of me, you know."

"I know," she said wryly. "My friend

Nancy assured me I was the last twenty-four-year-old virgin left on the face of the earth. I was a little afraid I would disappoint you." She raised her head to look up at him uncertainly. "Was I all right?"

His lips swooped down to kiss her with a gentleness that caused her throat to tighten with an aching tenderness. "Lord, you were fantastic, love," he said, his voice suspiciously husky. "I've never felt anything like that in my life. It was as if every part of you was holding me, loving me. I couldn't believe my luck."

"Neither could I," she said softly, her eyes twinkling impishly. "It's not every woman who's initiated into the intricacies of sex by such a notable practitioner as Lusty Lance. I should consider myself almost unique. I'm sure you don't usually waste that expertise on such unsophisticated quarry."

His brow wrinkled in a frown. "That's not amusing," he said curtly. "I told you that what we have is different. Now, be quiet and come here." He pressed her head back into the hollow of his shoulder, his arms tightening around her. "Did I ever tell you that I hate that Lusty Lance epithet?"

"No," she answered, nestling even closer. "Did I tell you that I think my own name is perfectly ghastly?"

"I believe you did mention something about it," he said, winding a lock of her hair around his finger. "I like it. It's as if I'm murmuring a love word every time I say it." His lips brushed lightly over her lids. "Honey sweet." His lips traveled to the lobe of her ear and nibbled delicately. "Honey soft." His lips moved to her mouth and his tongue entered to joust with her own in eager play. When their lips parted, he drew a shuddering breath. "Honey hot. I think I want to paint another picture."

Her eyes widened in surprise. "So soon?"

He chuckled. "Couldn't you tell by the number of canvases in my studio?" he asked softly. "I'm very prolific." One hand closed on her breast, his nail raking lightly over the nipple, sending a shiver of heat through her. "And I'm finding you a source of constant inspiration."

Honey found that she, too, was feeling more inspired by the moment, as his lips traveled down to her breast and his tongue flicked deliciously at the taut pink tip. "You're so damn beautiful, I want to *really* paint you, just as you are right now. Will you pose for me, Honey?"

She felt a sharp pain surge through her as she remembered what Alex had said about Lance's dislike of painting anyone with whom he was personally involved. Evidently she didn't fall into that category. Well, what could she expect? Lance had never pretended that he felt any lasting attachment for her. She must be satisfied with what he had to give.

"Why not?" she asked flippantly. "I can hardly complain about your making me notorious. You must have the most private collection of paintings in the entire world."

He started to say something, but she swiftly put her hand over his lips, silencing him. "On one condition."

He kissed her palm lingeringly before removing her hand from his lips. "And that is?"

Her hands reached up to draw his glossy, flamelike head back to her breast. "I find that I'm developing a few artistic tendencies myself," she said lightly. "I want to paint my own picture. Will you teach me how to do it?"

"Oh, yes, sweetheart." He chuckled, his blue eyes flickering. His teeth nibbled at one eager nipple. "First, you have to prepare the canvas."

And the lesson commenced.

It was late afternoon when she awoke, and the glowing rays of the sun were slanting through the window, softening the austerity of the room.

Honey stretched luxuriously, feeling delightfully lazy as she cast the denim coverlet aside. She felt a twinge of disappointment that Lance had left without waking her, but she firmly squashed the feeling. He was probably back in the studio again. She mustn't expect to compete with the pull of that particular mistress, though she had every intention of making herself a worthy adversary of any other possible rivals.

She showered quickly and washed her hair, grumbling at her shortsightedness in not bringing a blow dryer. Exposed to the salt air, her long hair would need continual care and frequent washing. Oh, well, she would just have to go outside and hope the sun would dry it before nightfall.

She slipped on a pair of navy-blue tailored shorts and a pale-blue tailored blouse, tying the tails carelessly under her breasts. She didn't bother with shoes, and when she left the cottage, the sand was a delicious cushion beneath her bare feet. The tide was coming in, and the surf licked at her toes as she strolled briskly along the shore, her hands combing through her hair occasionally, while the soft, gentle wind obligingly dried it.

It was almost sunset, and Honey paused for a moment to gaze with breathless admiration at the scarlet and violet glory that was reflected mirror-like in the placid sea.

"It's a magnificent picture, but I like the ones we paint together more."

She whirled to face Lance, an eager smile lighting her face. "So do I," she said softly. "I think we get the colors better."

Bathed in the rosy sunset glow, his skin took on a golden patina, and his hair glowed like a flame above the sapphire eyes. He was barefoot, too, she noticed, and he hadn't bothered to tuck the tail of his white shirt into his jeans, nor to button it.

"I thought you'd gone back to the studio," she said.

He shook his head, his face surprisingly grave. "I went for a long walk. I had some thinking to do."

She moved closer. "I'm glad you haven't gone back to work yet," she murmured, smiling at him beguilingly. "I was wondering if I could seduce you into giving me another lesson."

"The key word being 'seduce,' of course," he said, a flame beginning to flicker in the depths of his eyes. "What a delightfully insatiable wench you've become, Honey. Any more practice and you'll be giving *me* lessons."

She took a step nearer him, until her breasts were pressing against the bare hardness of his chest. "You didn't object this afternoon," she observed with a grin.

"No, I didn't, did I?" he asked thickly. "I couldn't get enough of you. I was even tempted to wake you before I left and love you again."

"Why didn't you?" she asked, her arms sliding up his chest and around his neck, her fingers curling in the crisp hair at its nape. Her lips brushed his chin, and he inhaled sharply.

Then he was jerking her arms from around his neck and thrusting her forcefully away from him. "Damn it, Honey, stay away from me," he said sharply. "This is difficult enough for me."

She gazed up at him in hurt bewilderment. "What's the matter?" she asked huskily, her blue eyes sparkling with unshed tears. She'd thought he'd been joking before about her aggressiveness, but perhaps there had been an element of sincerity beneath the raillery. She backed slowly away from him, her lashes lowered to veil the pain that the thought brought. "You'll have to forgive me," she said brightly, smiling with an effort. "I'm a little new at this. You'll have to let me know what's bad form and what isn't."

"Oh, Lord, now I've hurt you," he groaned, running his hand through his hair in frustration. "It's not like that. I'm not rejecting you, damn it."

"It sounds remarkably like it," she said, still not looking at him. "But you needn't apologize, Lance, I understand perfectly."

He took an impulsive step forward, reaching out for her. Then he stopped abruptly, and his hands fell to his sides. "Honey, you're driving me crazy," he said in an exasperated tone. "You know that I can scarcely keep my hands off of you. I proved that this afternoon. You're the most warmly responsive woman I've ever known. I'd be the last one ever to discourage you from spreading a little of that warmth in my direction."

"Then what's wrong?" she asked, her violet eyes lifting in puzzlement to meet his own. "If you want me, and I want you . . ."

"It's not that simple," he said, scowling. "You were a virgin."

Her mouth fell open in surprise. "After today, I think it's a little late to worry about that," she said dryly. "It certainly didn't appear to bother you too much earlier."

"Look, I know I acted like a selfish bastard," he said, frowning. "I guess I went a little crazy. You go to my head, love." He threw out his arms in frustration. "I never dreamed you weren't experienced. I thought you'd be on the pill."

"The pill?" she asked dazedly. "Is that what this is all about? You're worried about my getting pregnant?" She suddenly started to laugh, her face alight with amusement.

His scowl grew darker. "I'm glad you're finding it so damn funny," he said indignantly. "We're on an island, remember? I could call the mainland to have something flown in, but Alex and others might find out. I thought that would embarrass you. I was foolishly trying to protect you."

She shook her head, her lips curved in a tender smile. "I'm the one who is supposed to be protecting you," she reminded him gently. "Don't worry, Lance. I'm not."

"That's because you're so naive," he said roughly. "You should be worried, damn it. Why the hell aren't you?"

Because the thought of a little redheaded Scaramouche with sapphire eyes filled her with an aching yearning. Because a part of him would be better than nothing at all. Because she would love this complicated, quicksilver boy-man all the days of her life.

She shrugged. "I don't know why you're

so upset. There's no use worrying about something that may never happen." She grinned, her eyes twinkling. "We'll be here another few weeks, and I'll be darned if I'll live like a nun, now that I know what I'm missing." Then, as she saw the endearingly troubled expression on his face, she said gently, "I'm not fooling myself that this will be forever, Lance. Whatever happens, I won't hold you responsible. I waited twenty-four years for my first affair, and I fully expect to enjoy every minute of it."

"How very generous of you," he said, his lips tight, and for a moment she thought she saw a flicker of hurt in the depths of his eyes. "As ephemeral as you consider our affair to be, I still regard myself as being a little more than a ship that passes in the night. I think a portion of that decision rests with me."

"But you've already admitted that you have ambivalent feelings on that score," she said demurely, peering up at him through her lashes. She moistened her lips delicately with the tip of her tongue, knowing he was watching her compulsively. "I, however, am entirely determined and singleminded about the subject."

"Honey," he said warningly.

"I want to paint another picture, Lance,"

she said coaxingly, taking a step forward.

He took an involuntary step backward. "No, damn it. Not until I can take care of you."

"You always take care of me," she said softly, taking another step forward. "I've never felt so beautifully cosseted in my life as when I'm in your arms, Lance."

"God, I hoped you felt like that, Honey," he said huskily. "You're so sweet to love that it takes my breath away. I wanted you to feel like the treasure that you are."

Her hands went to the buttons on her blouse and began slowly to unfasten them. "Treasures are always more precious when they're used," she said softly. "Did you ever see how ugly and tarnished silver becomes when it's left in the cabinet? Don't leave me on the shelf, Lance." She shrugged out of the blouse and dropped it carelessly on the sand.

Lance's eyes were fixed on her breasts as her hands went to the front closure of her bra. "Where's the woman who was too modest to wear a bikini?" he asked wryly, moistening his dry lips with the tip of his tongue.

"The sun's gone down now, and you did invite me to go skinny-dipping with you."

"Somehow I don't think that's what you

have in mind," he said dryly.

She winked at him impishly. "Well, there are dips." She slipped out of the bra. "And then there are *dips*."

He drew a deep, ragged breath. "God, you're beautiful," he said hoarsely, his eyes on the full mounds with their taut pink rosettes. "You're making it very hard for me, love."

"That's the purpose of the entire exercise," she said, her lips quirking. She took a step closer to him. "Now, don't you think it's time that I had another lesson in the subtle nuances of color coordination?"

"Don't do this, Honey," he grated out, his hands clenching into fists at his sides. "I'm trying to do what's right, for once in my life." His eyes were fastened on one pink tantalizing nipple, and unconsciously he licked his lips again. "I can't stand much more of this. If you don't get away from me, so help me, I'll rape you."

She took another step closer until her bare breasts were brushing against his warm chest. "So rape me; I'll help you," she said flippantly, her violet eyes dancing mischievously. She stood on her tiptoes and kissed him with loving sweetness. "Love me, Lance."

He made a sound that was almost a guttural groan of hunger, deep in his throat, and his arms crushed her to him. His tongue entered to stroke with a savage desire that took her breath away. He drew her down to the sand, so that they were kneeling face to face, while his hands moved feverishly over the smooth silken line of her back. "I hope you know what you're doing, Honey," he muttered, as he pressed burning kisses over her face and throat. "You've made damn sure that I don't."

She was sliding the shirt from his shoulders and down his arms. "I know," she said, pressing her lips to his shoulder. "I know very well what I'm doing."

He was breathing raggedly, and she could feel the rapid throb of his heart beneath her lips. "There's one thing you've got to promise me, Honey," he said hoarsely as he pushed her down in the sand, his hands working at the fastening of her navy shorts. "No abortion." His expression was pale and stern in the dim light. "Whatever happens, no abortion. Okay?"

She smiled up at him tenderly. It was entirely what she would have expected of someone as vividly alive as Lance. How much he had yet to learn about her and the love she felt for him. "Okay," she agreed softly, pulling him down into her embrace. "Whatever happens, love."

SIX

The wind was tearing wildly at her hair and robbing her of breath as she and Lance ran the last few yards to the porch of the Folly. Lance didn't bother to knock, but threw open the door, bustled her into the foyer, and slammed the door behind them.

Honey was trying futilely to smooth her hair as she turned and gazed laughingly up at him. "You really know how to pick the time to accept a dinner invitation, Lance. That wind almost blew us away. I must look a complete mess."

"I like it," he said softly, his eyes running lingeringly over her tousled white-gold hair and equally windblown tailored cream slacks and chocolate silk blouse. "It makes you look very satisfyingly primitive," he added, smoothing his own rumpled hair. "Perhaps I should change the background in your painting. A Valkyrie should really have a storm setting to be really effective."

"Just so you don't insist on having me bare-breasted and wearing a horned helmet," Honey said dryly, making a face at him.

He shook his head ruefully. "I learned my lesson that first day I tried to paint you nude. I find you too much of a temptation in the buff, my proud beauty."

Her eyes twinkled teasingly. "I noticed you didn't get any work done that day. And I thought artists were supposed to regard their models in a purely objective light."

"Never purely," he said with a wicked grin. "Not when the model is you, Honey sweet. Objective? Perhaps in fifty years or so I might muster a little objectivity."

Honey inhaled sharply, feeling a flutter of delight deep in the heart of her. It was the first time in the two weeks they'd been on the island that he'd intimated that their affair was to be anything but fleeting. She didn't fool herself that Lance would make any lasting commitment to her.

The past weeks had been the happiest she'd ever known, and she felt she had grown closer to Lance Rubinoff than to anyone before in her life. Not only did they share a white-hot physical affinity that rocked them to their depths, but they'd found that they shared a gentle camaraderie that was amazing, considering the disparity in their upbringings. She was almost sure that Lance felt the golden ties that were being forged between them, but this was the first verbal indication he'd ever made that their idyll might extend beyond the confines of Londale's Folly.

Her face must have mirrored the glowing delight she was feeling, for his eyes were suddenly narrowed and intent, and he took an impulsive step toward her. "Honey," he said huskily, "let's go back to the cottage."

"Oh, no, you don't." Alex Ben Raschid's voice cut through the velvet sensual haze that was beginning to envelop them. Alex stood in the arched doorway of the living room. "I haven't been able to pry the two of you away from that seaside love nest since we arrived. I'm tired of my own company, damn it."

Honey could feel the hot color flood her cheeks, as she watched Ben Raschid stroll lazily toward them. Dressed in dark cords and a long-sleeved black shirt, no one could have looked more self-sufficient and less dependent than that sleek panther of a man.

Lance's expression was also plainly skeptical, as he took Honey's arm in a possessive clasp and turned to face Alex. "Nice to know we were missed," he said mockingly.

"However, I don't seem to remember you pounding down our door. Admit it, Alex, you've been so busy wheeling and dealing that you didn't even remember that we were alive."

"I refuse to admit any such thing," Alex replied, his lips quirking. "I would never have committed the *faux pas* of interrupting love's young dream without a good reason. *I* don't have an artistic temperament to excuse my rudeness."

"No, just that Ben Raschid arrogance," Lance murmured silkily. "And you seem to have overcome your scruples enough to send a note down with an invitation that was the equivalent of a royal command."

"Sheer desperation," Alex said, making a face. "I may have been able to tolerate my own company, but I wasn't about to fight off the Teutonic Terror on my own. She's been calling, wanting to speak to you, for the past three evenings." He looked at his watch. "She said she'd be calling you tonight at seven-thirty our time. Knowing Bettina's Germanic efficiency, that leaves you exactly three minutes to gird your loins for battle."

Lance gave him a look of utter disgust. "My God, Alex, couldn't you have told her that I was in Sedikhan? Clancy could have fobbed her off. Lord knows he's had enough practice."

Alex shook his head, a glint of amusement in his dark eyes. "She'd still track you down, with her usual bloodhound's persistence," he said. "It's a quality I rather admire. I thought she deserved at least to talk to you."

"Thanks," Lance said gloomily, running a distracted hand through the auburn hair that he'd so recently smoothed. "I'll do the same for you sometime."

"Teutonic Terror?" Honey asked, puzzled. "Who on earth are you talking about?"

"Baroness Bettina von Feltenstein," Lance replied absently, still scowling at Alex.

As if on cue, Justine appeared in the foyer. "Baroness von Feltenstein is on the phone for Prince Rubinoff," she announced quietly before disappearing once again toward the rear of the house.

Alex glanced at his watch. "She's thirty seconds early." His lips twitched. "Most reprehensible. Be sure to reprimand her, Lance." He gestured toward the door at the far end of the foyer. "You can take it in the library while I get Honey a drink."

Lance muttered a distinctly blue imprecation and strode quickly through the foyer, slamming the library door behind him.

Honey followed Alex to the bar at the far side of the room, slipped onto a yellow-

cushioned barstool, and watched distractedly as Alex went behind the bar.

"Ginger ale?" he inquired as he took two
glasses from beneath the bar and placed
them on the polished teak counter.

"You have a good memory," she said.
"Why is Lance so upset?" she persisted,
watching as he poured his own brandy and
replaced the crystal decanter beneath the
bar.

"She's his parents' choice for a blushing
bride," he explained. He came around the
bar and half sat, half leaned on the stool
next to her own. When he noticed Honey's
look of surprise, he added quickly, "Not
Lance's. He can barely stand the woman.
She's a bit too aggressive for his taste. He
just can't convince Bettina of that fact.
She's been so brainwashed that she can't
conceive why Lance doesn't want to marry
her and have a multitude of splendidly bred
Teutonic princelings."

"I see," Honey said slowly, looking down
at her glass to mask the sudden jolt of pain
she was feeling. "It must be very exasperating for him."

"I don't think you do see, Honey," he said
quietly. "I've never known Lance to do
anything he didn't want to do. He can't be
bulldozed into a state marriage unless that's

169

what he wants. I think you know Lance well enough to realize that's definitely not what he wants."

She looked up, and her eyes were bright with tears. "I haven't known Lance long enough to be that sure of him," she said quietly. "He's not the easiest person to understand. About ninety percent of Lance Rubinoff is beneath the surface."

"Well, if it's any comfort to you, I think you have a better chance at probing those depths than any other woman has had," Alex said gently. "The man is obviously crazy about you."

Honey felt a surge of hope. "It is a comfort to me," she said honestly, giving him a grateful smile. "Thank you for telling me, Alex."

"The woman is completely impossible!" Lance exclaimed explosively, striding into the room and heading immediately for the bar. "She's a ranting lunatic." He poured himself a double. "And she has the persistence of a bloody bulldog with a fresh bone!"

"I gather that you didn't convince her that you were quite happy with your single state?" Alex asked, arching a mocking brow.

"My God, when that woman begins quoting bloodlines, she makes me feel like a blasted stud!" Lance said disgustedly, down-ing half his drink in one swallow.

"Well, she can only judge by your past performance." Alex grinned. "The results may not be evident, but the inclination certainly was. Is she going to pay us a visit to try to further her cause?"

"Probably," Lance replied gloomily. "I did everything I could to discourage her, but it was like talking to a post."

Suddenly Honey couldn't take any more. Couldn't they talk about anything but that high-bred vamp? She slipped off the stool and wandered over to the French windows, where sheets of rain were pounding against the panes. "We're going to be drowned before we get back to the cottage," she said, with an effort at lightness. "This doesn't look like a pleasant little tropical shower."

"You won't be going back to the cottage tonight," Alex said calmly, and when she whirled to face him with a surprised excla-mation, he gave a resigned sigh. "I forgot how primitive you are down at the cottage. You don't even have a radio, do you? You're right, this isn't just a shower. It's been of-ficially labeled a tropical storm." His lips tightened grimly. "If it stays in the Gulf much longer, it will probably escalate to a full-fledged hurricane. At any rate, you won't have to worry about any surprise visits from Bettina for the next day or so."

"Thank God," Lance said emphatically, taking another drink. "I'm grateful for small favors."

"I sent Nate down to the cottage to pack your belongings and bring them up here," Alex said. "Until the storm passes, you'll have to remain as my guests. The cottage will be completely flooded in a few hours. I've told Justine to prepare a guest room."

"What about Lance's paintings?" Honey asked worriedly.

"They'll be quite safe," Alex said soothingly. "I told Nate to wrap them carefully in tarpaulin before trying to transport them."

Honey breathed a sigh of relief. She should have known that Alex would take every care. He valued Lance's work almost as much as she did.

"They should be in the library by now, if you want to examine them for possible damage," he continued, turning to Lance, as he finished his drink and set the empty glass on the bar.

Lance shook his head. "Nate's pretty careful. I'm sure they're all right," he said carelessly, finishing his own drink. "I'll check them after dinner."

"Perhaps you should take a look now,"

Honey urged, her brow creased in a frown. "You wouldn't want to chance having any of them ruined." She cast an uneasy glance at the rain pounding against the window. "There can't be much time left."

Lance's lips curved in a cynical smile. "I can always paint another one."

Honey expelled a deep breath of sheer frustration. "I won't even honor that idiocy with a reply," she said between her teeth. Then, unable to resist, she burst out, "You're not some hack painter, damn it. Everything you do is *important*."

Alex gave a low whistle. "I think I detect the trace of a long-standing argument," he remarked, straightening. "If you'll excuse me, I believe I'll go to the library and make a number of completely unnecessary phone calls. Justine will let us know when dinner is ready."

"You needn't leave, Alex," Honey said tautly. "I know when I'm beating a dead horse. Where did you say the guest room is? I believe I'll go upstairs and freshen up."

"It's the first door on the left," Alex said promptly, settling back on the stool. "And if you're not going to argue, I believe I'll stay and have another drink." He cast an inquiring glance at his cousin. "Lance?"

"Why not?" Lance asked, his eyes fixed

broodingly on Honey's back as she walked swiftly toward the door. "Lord, save me from obstinate women."

That the charge was leveled at her as well as the absent Teutonic Terror was more than clear, and Honey felt a little stab of hurt along with her annoyance and distress. She didn't answer, but swept regally from the room and up the stairs. There was very little she could do with her slightly tousled appearance, but if she hadn't gotten out of that room, there would have been the argument Alex had predicted.

Alex was right. Their argument was of long standing, the only one to disturb the golden tranquility of their time together. Why couldn't the man see that he needed that God-given talent he'd been blessed with to be recognized? Such great creativity couldn't be hidden away in a studio, like the canvases that Lance had shoved carelessly away in the closet.

She stopped short on the top step. Oh, God, surely Nate had gotten those paintings out of the closet? Without thinking, she whirled and flew back down the steps and through the foyer to the library. Nate was careful, as Lance had said, but he must have been in a tremendous hurry to get all their belongings together and up to the Folly before the deluge. What if he'd failed to check the closet?

She burst into the library, paying no attention this time to the portrait of Karim Ben Raschid, which subtly made the room its own. The canvases were stacked against the wall, carefully wrapped in the waterproof tarpaulin. There were so many, but were they all there? She hurriedly tore the tarpaulin off the pictures, giving each one a cursory glance. She had grown to know them all in the last weeks, as if they were beloved children. They were children, in a way. Lance's children, product of the genius he refused to acknowledge. Damn, why couldn't she remember which paintings had been in the closet? Perhaps Nate had brought them after all.

No, wait, where was the *Hidden Lagoon*? She remembered asking Lance how he'd gotten that curiously intimate effect, with the sheltering trees surrounding the mystic, tranquil waters. Frantically she went through the canvases again. Maybe she'd just overlooked it. Let it be here, please. It wasn't! Nate had missed it. And how many others that she couldn't recall at the moment? Lance's beautiful children.

No, damn it. She wouldn't let them be taken away by a stupid freak of nature!

Her movements were almost automatic as she swiftly spread out several tarpaulins on the floor and folded them carefully. She tucked the bulky bundle under her arm and left the library, running toward the front door. She had no time to get a coat or other rain gear. It would only protect her for a few minutes, anyway, in a torrential storm like this one.

She couldn't have been more right on that score. The rain hit her like a blow, and she was drenched to the skin in seconds. The wind was blowing water before it with such force that Honey had to struggle to keep her feet on the palm-bordered path down the hill to the beach.

The path was a muddy quagmire, as she half ran, half slid down the incline. The trip that should have taken her five minutes took her a full fifteen, and by the time she reached the beach, she was almost panicky. The storm was moving with such ominous swiftness. Would the cottage be flooded already when she reached it?

It was impossible to see the cottage until she was almost upon it, so blinding were the solid sheets of rain pounding at her. She stumbled over the front stoop and had to catch her balance by grabbing at the jamb of the front door, or she would have fallen to her knees. The stoop was already completely flooded, and water was running under the front door when she threw it open and staggered into the cottage.

She wasted scarcely a glance on the stripped living-dining area, but ran immediately to the studio. That, too, was stripped and bare. It was clear that Nate had salvaged all of the paintings he'd noticed, but when she threw open the door of the closet, Honey saw what she'd expected. Propped in a shadowy corner were three canvases. One was fairly small, but the other two were good-sized, and she immediately recognized one as the *Hidden Lagoon.* She gave a sigh of relief, and lifted the precious canvases carefully out of the closet, after meticulously checking the shelves to make sure she hadn't missed anything.

The water was washing under the door of the studio now, and Honey knew she didn't have much time. She quickly unfolded the tarpaulins. She'd purposely taken more than she'd thought she would need. Now, after her wild journey down the hill, she was glad of the extra protection. It would be ironic if, after all her trouble, the paintings were damaged on her way back to the Folly. Keeping a wary eye on the seawater that was rushing under the door in a constant tide now, she quickly wrapped each painting in a double thickness of tarpaulin and then tied them all together under the protection of a larger one. By the time she finished, a thin stream of water was washing around her kneeling figure, and she hurriedly picked up the paintings, hugging them to her breasts as she opened the studio door. The water gushed into the room with a little swoosh, and Honey could feel a thrill of sheer panic as she fought her way to the front door through the knee-deep water. If it was this bad in the cottage, what must it be like outside?

It was like jumping into the ocean itself when she stepped off the stoop. The pounding waves were more than waist deep, and it was impossible to keep the paintings entirely out of the salt water as she struggled to make her way toward the path, whose lower reaches were now invisible beneath the stormy surf. Her breath was coming in sharp, painful gasps as she finally tore herself from the deadly clinging waters, which threatened to suck her back into their embrace with each swirling pull of the pounding waves.

Honey staggered drunkenly to the side of the path and leaned against a tall palm, trying to get her breath. There was a sharp stitch in her side, and she felt almost dizzy with exhaustion as she clutched the bole of the tree with one arm and the paintings in the other. She'd never dreamed there was so much water in the world. For a while she couldn't determine what was sea and what wasn't, so thick was the blanket of rain that surrounded her.

The sea was again licking hungrily at her ankles, she noticed numbly. How high must she climb to escape its reach? She released her grip on the tree, tightened her arms around the paintings, and began to fight her way up the path. It couldn't be much farther, could it? It seemed as if she'd traveled miles already. She stumbled and fell to her knees in the mud of the trail, and for a moment she stayed there, too weary to move, gathering her resources for the next effort.

"Honey! My God, I could murder you!"

She raised her head slowly, not even surprised to see Lance standing on the path in front of her. He was very wet, she thought numbly. His jeans were clinging to the strong line of his thighs like a second skin, the dark copper of his skin visible through the wet cotton of his shirt. She couldn't see his features through the dense curtain of rain, but his tone was enraged.

Great. That was all she needed at the moment, to have Lance furious with her. Well, she'd better face it standing up. She was starting to struggle to her feet, when Lance suddenly pulled her up, shaking her like a rag doll. That was just what she felt like, she thought dazedly. Her legs were certainly stuffed with cotton, for they gave way, and she felt herself falling. Then she was scooped up and held close to Lance's chest, while a string of obscenities issued from him in a strange, broken voice.

"Calm down, Lance," Alex's voice came out of the darkness somewhere over Lance's shoulder. "You're not making it any easier for her."

"I don't want to make it any easier for her. I could beat her. Just look at her, damn it!" Lance said harshly. "Take those blasted canvases from her and get rid of them, will you? She's got them in a death grip."

"No!" Honey gasped sharply, her arms tightening possessively on the paintings.

Alex was beside them now, and his voice was as gentle as Lance's had been harsh. "Let me have them, Honey. I'll take good care of them."

Yes, Alex would take good care of them, she thought tiredly. Her hands loosened, and the paintings were lifted from her clasp. Her arms felt oddly empty as they fell to her sides. "Yes, you take care of them, Alex," she said. "I'm so tired." She relaxed drowsily and then nestled closer in Lance's arms. There was an odd sound that was half growl and half sob beneath her ear, but she didn't hear it, as she fell peacefully asleep.

Honey's next conscious awareness was of being lowered into a tub of warm bubbly water that jolted her from sleep to a disgruntled wakefulness.

"Not more water," she protested disgustedly, opening sleepy eyes to glare indignantly at Lance. "I'm practically pruney now."

"Too bad!" he said, rolling up the sleeves of his wet cream shirt with one hand while he steadied her with the other. "You'll just have to bear with it. At the moment, you're so muddy, you look more like a tar baby than a Valkyrie. Now, be quiet while I get you cleaned up and into bed."

She opened her lips to reply, but they were immediately covered by a ruthless hand wielding a soapy washcloth, and she was forced to shut them abruptly. Lance's movements were far from gentle as he scrubbed her from head to toe, until she glowed pink and saucy as a baby. Then he washed her hair with equal impersonality and cool efficiency, his expression granite-hard and guarded. An expression that reminded her of Alex. Alex?

"The paintings!" she exclaimed, suddenly sitting upright in the tub. "Are they all right?"

"Alex said that would be the first thing you'd ask," he said, grabbing a bath sheet from the towel rack. "You'll be happy to know that they were in perfect condition when Alex unwrapped them." He stood up and lifted her out of the tub and wrapped her in the voluminous towel. "Which is a hell of a lot better than you. What in Hades happened to your knees?"

"My knees?" Honey asked vaguely. Looking down, she noticed with surprise that they were both badly bruised, and one had a ragged cut across the kneecap. "I must have done it when I fell in the mud." She frowned in puzzlement. "I don't remember its hurting when I did it."

"You were probably in shock," Lance said roughly, briskly rubbing her hair dry. "You're still not very coherent. Are you sure you didn't hit your head out there?"

She slowly shook her head, frowning at him crossly. "I'm perfectly coherent," she said resentfully, "though I don't know how you can judge. You haven't been letting me say a word."

"Silence is golden and, in your case, a good deal safer," Lance muttered between his teeth as he scooped her up and carried her into the adjoining bedroom. He sat her on the edge of the bed and left her for a moment to fetch the portable hair dryer from the dresser across the room. "It's a little late for you to turn verbose. Now, shut up while I get your hair dry. You'll be lucky if you come out of this without pneumonia."

She opened her lips to answer but she was interrupted again, this time by the shrill roar of the dryer, as Lance proceeded to dry her hair.

Honey sat obediently silent under the warm blast of air, but her temper was slowly burning. Lance acted as if she'd committed a major crime instead of merely trying to salvage a few paintings. She hadn't expected him to be grateful, but he didn't have to be so damned churlish. Even Alex had been more gentle with her than this red-haired bear of a man.

Lance clicked off the dryer and threw it carelessly on the lime-cushioned empress chair by the bed. "It's still a little damp, but it will have to do." He turned and strode toward the bathroom. "Get under the covers and keep warm until I get out of the shower." His hands were rapidly unbuttoning the sodden cream shirt. "But don't go to sleep — I still have to care for those knees."

Honey stood up, clutching the bath sheet firmly to keep it from slipping. "You needn't bother," she said coolly. "I'll attend to them myself. I'll be dressed for dinner by the time you get out of the shower."

"Dinner!" His laugh was a harsh bark as he pulled off the wet shirt and tossed it on the carpet. "We'll forget about dinner this evening. Thanks to your stupidity, I don't think any of us are in the mood for a congenial meal." He disappeared into the bathroom, slamming the door behind him.

Honey glared belligerently at the door before stalking angrily to the Korean wedding chest that served as a bureau in the corner of the room. So she was not only in Lance's bad books, but was to be sent to bed without any supper! She wasn't in the mood for a social dinner either, but she was hungry, damn it.

She snatched the first nightgown she saw in the drawer, and noticed with satisfaction that it was a shapeless, thigh-length cotton nightshirt with a friendishly smiling Garfield the Cat on the breast. She certainly didn't want Lance to think she was trying to seduce him into a better humor. He was entirely in the wrong, and she would make sure that he was aware of that fact. Two minutes later she had folded back the lime-and-white bamboo-patterned spread on the bed and slipped between the sheets, plumping the pillow with furious energy and pulling the sheets up to her chin before settling down to wait grimly for Lance.

When he did stride back into the bedroom, with only a white towel draped about his hips, she felt a treacherous wavering of her resolve. Why did the man have to be so damn sexy? she wondered gloomily. He was all sleek copper muscle and virile grace as he moved toward her, and she felt a familiar stirring in her loins, which she tried to disregard. His face was still grimly set, she noticed sourly, and she girded herself for the battle to come.

"Did you take care of your knees?" he asked tersely as he sat down on the side of the bed.

"Of course I did," she lied defensively, her glance sliding guiltily away from him. She'd been so incensed by his arrogance and unjust anger that she'd completely forgotten. Her injuries weren't all that bad anyway.

"Fine!" he said curtly, ripping off the towel. He punched the button on the lamp on the bedside table, and the room was suddenly in darkness. She felt the mattress depress as he slid beneath the sheets and settled himself on his side of the bed. "Good night."

Good night? Was that all? How dare he be so cool and unconcerned, after the way he'd treated her? She was the injured party, and in more ways than physical, yet he was calmly going to sleep without giving her a chance to air her grievances. Could anything be more infuriating? Well, perhaps "calm" was the wrong word to use. Even across that icy expanse of bed, she could detect the tenseness of his muscles as he lay there, and a taut aura of leashed emotion was crackling about him like a live wire. It was clear that he was still angry with her and was letting her know it in no uncertain terms. Tonight was the first time since they'd become lovers that she wasn't sleeping in his arms. Not that it mattered to her if he was as remote and cold as the Himalayas, she assured herself. It was just that she had become used to that warm, loving embrace enfolding her, and she felt a little lonely without it. Suddenly there was a rumbling deep in her stomach. That did it! She'd had enough!

Throwing back the covers, she jumped out of bed and strode purposefully toward the louvered closet.

"Where the hell are you going?" Lance's surprised voice came out of the darkness behind her.

"I'm hungry," Honey said belligerently. "I may not be considered worthy of dinner, but you can't object if I go downstairs and raid the refrigerator. You may aspire to being a starving artist, but I'm just a pragmatic private investigator. I want something to eat!"

The light immediately flicked on behind her, and she riffled through the closet for a robe as Lance hissed an imprecation. She ignored him, pulling a white terry-cloth robe off a hanger and slamming the door behind her as she turned around.

"Garfield?"

"What?" she asked, frowning crossly at him. Then she followed his eyes down to the leering cat on her breast. "I like him," she said defensively. "He has character." She struggled into the terry-cloth robe. "And feelings! And that's more than some people I know."

"Garfield," he repeated in wonder. And suddenly he began to laugh. "My Lord, Garfield!"

She planted her hands on her hips and glared at him. It wasn't enough that this maddening man had been growling at her like a surly lion; now he actually had the gall to laugh at her!

Her fury only seemed to amuse him more, for he now dissolved in laughter as he gazed at her cross face and belligerent stance. "I fail to see what's so amusing," she said icily.

"I've never had a cat leer at me from the breast of a Valkyrie with such a royal bearing," he gasped, wiping his eyes on a fold of the sheet. "You'll forgive me if it struck me as funny."

"I'm not the one who's royal," she spat, her violet eyes flashing. "I'm just a poor humble serf. It's Your Highness who has the privilege of being rude and sulky and abusive and completely unreasonable!" She was practically sputtering by the time she finished, and was pacing restlessly back and forth. "And besides that, you're trying to starve me to death!"

"I'm sorry," he said, his blue eyes dancing. "I can see that last sin outweighs all the others." His lips curved in a tender smile. "Come back to bed, Honey. I want to see if that pussycat knows how to purr as well as spit at me."

"If I did, I'd be tempted to do more than

spit," she said through her teeth, turning and striding furiously toward the door.

Her hand had only closed around the knob when she felt herself being scooped up and carried kicking and struggling back to the bed. She was dropped on the counterpane, and he immediately followed her down, pinning her arms above her head and throwing a hard thigh over her flailing legs to hold her immobile. "Now," he said, smiling down at her furious face. "Purr for me, Honey."

It was too much after all she'd gone through tonight. Two tears suddenly brimmed and ran slowly down her face.

They had a galvanic effect on the man grinning impishly down at her. He stiffened as if she'd struck him, and his face looked almost frightened. "No!" he ordered sharply. "Don't do that to me. Stop it, do you hear?"

She didn't know what he meant, but there was seemingly no way she could stop the tears, now that they had started. "Nothing you could do would make me cry," she said fiercely. "I'm just angry."

"That's what I wanted, but you weren't supposed to cry," he said accusingly. His eyes were haunted as he looked down at her. "You musn't do that, damn it. You'll ruin everything."

189

She stared up at him in complete bewilderment. He was totally irrational. "I don't know what you're talking about," she said tremulously. "You're not making sense."

"Never mind!" he said huskily. "It's too late now anyway. I can feel myself breaking into a hundred pieces inside." She was released with dizzying suddenness, and his arms went around her in a bone-crushing embrace that almost squeezed the breath out of her. He rolled over, holding her in a clasp that was curiously sexless, for all its possessive strength. "Don't move. Don't say anything. Just let me hold you. Okay?"

"All right," she answered faintly. Her anger had vanished when she'd heard that first note of desperation in his voice. She couldn't have moved even if she'd wanted to, so convulsive was that iron grasp. "Lance?" she asked uncertainly. "Please tell me what's wrong."

"Everything would have been fine if you hadn't cried," he muttered throatily into her hair. "I could have held it off until you went to sleep."

"Held what off?" Honey asked bewilderedly. Then, incredibly, she thought she was beginning to understand. His body was shaking and trembling against her like that of a malaria victim. "My God, Lance, what's wrong? Are you sick?"

"I'm sick, all right," he growled with a short mirthless laugh. "I'm so scared, I feel like I'm going to fall apart. I've been frightened out of my mind since we first discovered you were gone tonight." His arms tightened. "Why the hell didn't you come to us instead of running off on your own? Do you know what kind of risk you ran going back to the cottage in a storm like that? You almost died, damn it. You had no right to take a chance like that over something as trivial as those lousy paintings."

"They're not lousy," she denied automatically. "They're as brilliant as your other work. I guess I didn't think about anything but saving the paintings, when I found they weren't with the others."

"Why the hell would you do something so incredibly stupid for a few daubs of paint on the canvas?" he asked throatily.

"They were part of you," she said simply. "I couldn't let them be destroyed." Her lips brushed back and forth caressingly on the tautness of his cheek. Her tone was gently teasing as she continued, "I was hired to guard you, remember? I'd have been remiss in my duty if I'd let anything happen to such an important part of your life."

"So you almost destroyed yourself instead," he said fiercely.

"I knew there wasn't much time." She was fighting to free herself from his embrace. It was terrible to feel so helpless when she wanted so desperately to hold him in her arms and comfort him. Then her arms were sliding around him and drawing him even closer with a fierce possessiveness.

"You were right there," he said bitterly. "Ten minutes later, and you wouldn't have stood a chance. I knew when we were racing down that hill after you that the odds were you'd already been swept away, that I might never see you again. I nearly went crazy," he whispered huskily. The words were muffled, but they held an odd note of wonder. "You cared that much about them?"

"I cared that much," she answered quietly. She was stroking his hair with an almost maternal tenderness. "Don't you think it's time to admit that you feel the same way about your work? You know it would have torn you apart to have anything happen to those paintings."

He raised his head, and she inhaled sharply as she saw the torment in his face and the blazing emotion in his sapphire eyes. "It wasn't worth risking you," he said fiercely. "Nothing's worth that. Promise

192

you'll never do a thing like that again."

Honey felt a sudden surge of joy that was like the warmth of home fires burning bright. "I promise," she said thickly, blinking back the tears.

His head lowered slowly, until he was just a breath away. "I've never felt like that before," he said softly. "I've always been able to hide behind laughter and cynicism when anything has come too close to me. But it wouldn't work tonight, Honey." He kissed her with such lingering sweetness that she felt her throat ache with tenderness. "You've become too important to me. I don't think I could stand it if I lost you now." He buried his face once more in the thick silk of her hair. "Honey?"

"Yes?" she answered dreamily. Surely that last inarticulate murmur could be considered something of a commitment?

His words were oddly jerky. "If it means that much to you, I'll have a show." He heard her sharply indrawn breath, and went on quickly. "But you've got to promise to stay with me after we leave the island. I won't go through that phony charade alone." His voice was tinged with bitterness. "I know you look on this little island idyll as a purely temporary liaison, but if you want me to exhibit, you'll have to restrain your eagerness to get back to your sleuthing."

Where had he gotten the absurd idea that she was eager to leave him? She vaguely remembered making some comment that she didn't expect any permanence in their relationship but that had been to lessen *his* feeling of responsibility.

"But Lance —" she started, but he quickly raised his head and covered her lips with his own.

"No, you can't talk me out of it," he said when he lifted his head. "You'll have to stay and give me moral support or it's no go."

"Well, I suppose I do have a responsibility to the art world," she said liltingly, her lips curving in an impish grin. "I guess I could stick around and hold your hand until you see how right I am and how absurdly stupid you've been. Who's going to care a hundred years from now if you were a prince or a ditch digger, when those experts are gazing raptly at your paintings in the Louvre?"

"Who indeed?" Lance echoed, a reluctant smile tugging at the corners of his lips. "We'll be lolling on adjoining clouds, and you'll look down and nudge me and say: 'See, I told you so.' "

"I hate people who say, I told you so," Honey said, making a face at him. "I'd never be so crass." Then her face sobered. "You won't be sorry, Lance."

"I'm glad one of us is so confident," he said wryly. "I guess only time will tell which one of us is right. I'll let Alex know that he can make arrangements with the Parke-Bernet Galleries. He's been after me for years. At least he'll be happy."

"Because he has the good sense to recognize genius when he sees it," Honey replied promptly. "And, like all good businessmen, he abhors a wasted talent."

"So do I," Lance said, his eyes twinkling. "Which is why I have no intention of wasting yours, sweetheart." His hand reached up to weigh her breast in his palm. "Are you sure you're hungry?" he asked wistfully.

"I'm sure," she said emphatically, despite the tiny responsive thrill she was feeling at his touch.

"I was afraid you were," he said morosely. "I guess we'd better go down and raid that refrigerator. It's obvious you're not going to let me seduce you until I satisfy the inner woman." He gave her a teasing kiss, his face alight with laughter. "And then, my love, I'm going to make sure that the inner woman satisfies me!"

SEVEN

The sun was shining brightly, and Honey felt as if she were glowing with a brilliance that could rival its warmth, as she skipped out on the terrace and took her place at the table.

Alex glanced up from the official-looking document he'd been examining with a scowl, and his expression relaxed into a warm smile that miraculously softened the hardness of his features. "Well, good morning. I take it that all is well with your world this fine day?" he drawled, throwing the paper carelessly on the breakfast table beside his plate. He reached for the coffee carafe and poured her coffee and refilled his own cup. "Where's Lance this morning?"

"Justine is taking some coffee up to that improvised studio you created for him," Honey said, taking a sip of her coffee. "He wanted to get to work changing the background of my portrait to a storm setting."

She smiled mischievously at him. "He was most displeased with you for not having the cottage cleaned up by now so that we could move back down to the beach. He says the light is much better there."

"Ungrateful wretch," Alex said. "It's only been three days since the storm, and the cottage was a complete disaster. We don't have unlimited manpower on this island, you know. Nate's working as fast as he can."

"I know," Honey said tranquilly, reaching for a warm croissant and buttering it liberally. "And so does Lance, when he thinks about it. He's just impatient to get on with his work." She looked up, violet eyes dancing. "He has great respect for your drive and initiative and wishes you'd channel a little toward the cottage cleanup."

Alex shook his head wryly. "I suppose I'll have to phone the mainland and have some help flown out. I learned a long time ago that that red-haired demon refuses to give up when he wants something." One dark brow arched mockingly. "I guess you've discovered that too."

Honey felt the warm color surge to her cheeks. "Yes," she answered quietly, her eyes glowing softly. "I've found that out."

There was a curiously gentle flicker in the face of the man opposite her before it was masked by the usual guarded cynicism. "You may tell Lance that I'll be as glad to get rid of him as he will be to go," he said lightly. "It's not easy for a man of my proclivities to be odd man out in this garden of Eden the two of you have created for yourselves."

Honey's eyes flew up to meet his. "Have we made you feel that?" she asked, stricken. "Alex, I'm so sorry. How rude you must think us."

"Not rude, just crazy about each other," Alex said dryly. "I can't fault your manners." He pulled a face. "Though Lance could have been a little less blatantly content in front of a man in my celibate state. I'm not used to being an observer instead of a participant."

That was definitely an understatement, from what Lance had told her of Alex's marathon sexual activities. He was extremely highly sexed, and required a woman more often than most. Honey had been so involved with her own concerns that she had never questioned why Alex had voluntarily arranged his stay at Londale's Folly with no willing female to alleviate the abstinence of the past weeks. It must have been as difficult as he'd said, to watch Lance and her together.

"We've been very selfish and inconsiderate, haven't we, Alex? Will you forgive us?" Honey asked contritely.

"I will," he said with a mocking grin. "But only because my ordeal is finally at an end. I've imported some company for myself for a few days." He glanced casually at his watch. "In fact, the helicopter should be arriving any minute now."

"Company?" Honey asked, puzzled. Then she felt a chill of apprehension run through her. "The baroness?"

His brows lifted in surprise. "Bettina? Good heavens, no! The redhead from the Starburst."

Honey relaxed and grinned teasingly. "Oh yes, the inventive one who's really a Scandinavian blonde. Does she have a name?"

"Leona Martell," he supplied, rising to his feet. "Would you like to come down to the landing pad and meet her?"

"Why not?" she asked. She pushed back her chair and stood up. "Lance won't even miss me until this afternoon, when he finishes the background."

"Then I'll take advantage of your charming company while I may," Alex said, gesturing grandly for her to precede him.

Leona Martell was certainly as alluring as

Alex had said, Honey thought a little later as she watched him place his hands on the waist of the tiny but voluptuous redhead to swing her out of the helicopter to the pad. Redhead or not, she appeared to be as passionate as even the most demanding man might require, melting into Alex's arms and pulling his head down to kiss him lingeringly.

Alex was more than enthusiastic in returning the embrace, Honey observed with amusement. When he did lift his head to see her grinning at him, he pulled the redhead closer and winked impishly over the top of her head. Honey giggled irrepressibly, and Alex's smile widened as he turned the redhead around to introduce her.

"Honey, I'd like you to meet Leona Martell. Honey Winston, Leona," he said as he waved permission to the helicopter pilot to take off. "Leona is a law student at Rice University, Honey."

"How do you do, Miss Martell," Honey said politely, over the roar of the rotors as the pilot started the engine. If this gorgeous redhead was a law student, then she must be an extremely well-to-do one. Those sky-blue slacks and ecru silk blouse practically screamed haute couture, and her rich red, curly hair had been styled and cut by a master.

The admiration was evidently mutual, for Honey's words were acknowledged with a distinctly vague pleasantry, while the red-head wistfully eyed Honey's long, silver blond hair. "My hair used to be almost that color," she said. "People used to stop and stare at me in the street."

"I'm sure they still do," Honey said politely. "You're a very beautiful woman, Miss Martell. Many men prefer redheads, no matter what they say in the song."

"I'll vouch for that," Alex said, carelessly touching a shimmering red curl at her nape.

To Honey's amazement, the remark was met by a bitterly resentful glance. It was so swift that it only flickered and then was gone, replaced by a dulcet sweetness. "Then that's all that's important, darling," Leona said softly. "I only recently had it done, and I suppose I'm not used to it yet. I've been trying to decide whether to keep it." She turned with a forced smile to Honey. "What do you think?" she asked brightly. "Would you dye that lovely hair, Miss Winston?"

Honey shook her head. "I'm afraid not," she said quietly. "But then, I couldn't afford to keep it as lovely as yours."

Alex's arm slid around the redhead's

waist. "Let's go up to the house and persuade Justine to make us a fresh pot of coffee," he suggested softly, his dark gaze
lingering intimately on her. He glanced up
at Honey inquiringly. "Honey?"

She shook her head ruefully. She had an
idea that Alex had more than coffee on his
mind at the moment, and that she might
find herself very much a third wheel. "I
don't think so," she said. "I believe I'll go
down to the cottage and see what progress
Nate is making on the cleanup. I'll see you
at lunch, perhaps."

"Perhaps," Alex echoed in a silken murmur that caused Honey to smother a grin
as she waved cheerfully and set off down
the path to the beach.

She had no intention of going down to
the cottage and harrying poor Nate. It was
very likely that Alex had been giving him a
difficult enough time in the past few days.
It was almost an hour later, when she was
strolling barefoot in the cove, that she saw
the ship. At first she thought it was a trick
of the light. The dazzle of the sun on the
water sometimes created strange mirages.
Honey stopped and shaded her eyes curiously, expecting to see a cargo ship or tanker
on its way to Houston's ship channel. Her
brow creased in a puzzled frown. Surely that

white dot on the horizon was too small to be either of those. It looked more like a small launch, and it didn't seem to be moving. It appeared to be rocking gently on the quiet waves as if it were at anchor. As if it were waiting. She tried to shake off the uneasiness that flooded her as she turned and began to walk slowly back toward the path that led to the Folly. How foolish to get upset over a launch that would probably be gone in an hour or two. It was more than likely just an innocent fishing party.

Yet it was an odd coincidence that the launch should anchor here, at the only cove that offered access to the island. A little too odd. Honey's stride quickened instinctively, keeping pace with her thoughts. That was the second out-of-the-ordinary occurrence today. First had been the arrival of Leona Martell, and now the launch waiting on the horizon. Waiting for what?

There couldn't be a connection, could there? Leona Martell had come at Alex's invitation. Still, something nagged at Honey. There was something not quite right about Leona Martell. Honey had been subconsciously aware of something amiss since she'd met her.

She skidded to a halt and inhaled sharply. Her hair! It was obvious that Leona Martell had liked being a blonde. Her expression had been frankly envious when she'd seen Honey's hair, and then there had been that strange resentful glance she had thrown at Alex. Why would a natural blonde who was very well satisfied with her coloring suddenly dye her hair red?

"Oh, my God!" Honey breathed, her eyes widening in horror. Then she was flying up the path to the Folly. She burst through the front door and took the steps to the second floor two at a time and then dashed down the corridor to the improvised studio where Lance was working.

He looked up vaguely as she burst into the room. "Lance," she said, trying to get breath enough to speak. "Alex told me once that almost everyone in your immediate circle knew of his passion for redheads, that it was practically a standing joke. Is that true?"

"What?" he asked absently, his gaze returning to the easel. "Yes, of course it's true."

"Oh, no!" she moaned frantically, and turned and raced from the room and down the corridor to Alex's room. How criminally stupid of her not to have made the connection at once. Since she'd come to the island, she had forgotten everything but Lance.

She'd even been rocked by the blissful serenity of their relationship into forgetting her purpose for being here. She prayed that she'd remembered in time.

She burst into Alex's room and frantically scanned the apparently empty master suite, before she noticed the door ajar at the far end of the room. There was only the sound of running water, yet it was enough to send a chill through her. How terribly easy it would be to drown in a bathtub a man who was exposed and vulnerable. Had it happened already? She tore across the bedroom and threw open the door.

Alex was lying in the center of a huge, blue-veined marble sunken tub that could well have graced one of his ancestor's seraglios, and he looked up in stunned amazement as Honey bolted into the room.

Honey gave him a quick, relieved glance, her attention concentrated on the woman on top of him.

"No!" she cried sharply, and the redhead looked over her shoulder with the same shocked surprise Alex had shown. But she only had time for that one glance, before Honey jumped into the tub with them. She grabbed Leona quickly in a neck lock and jerked her away from Alex with one swift motion.

"Honey, for God's sake, stop it!" Alex shouted, struggling into a sitting position.

She paid no attention, for the redhead was struggling with surprising strength for one who appeared so fragile, and Honey needed all her expertise to subdue her. Who would have believed a nude body could be so slippery? It was like trying to handle a greased pig.

"Honey, so help me God, I'm going to murder you," Alex roared. "Let her go, damn it."

There was only one way to put an end to this. She spun the redhead around and stepped back a pace for leverage and then followed through with a right cross to the woman's jaw.

The redhead gave a guttural grunt, and her blue eyes slowly glazed over. Honey caught her as she started to slump, and heaved her out of the water onto the marble floor.

"Damn you, Honey," Alex groaned, covering his eyes with his hand. "Why the hell didn't you listen to me?"

"I can't talk right now, Alex," she said, levering herself out of the tub. "I've got to find something to tie her up with before she regains consciousness." She was gone before he could answer, but returned an instant later with a cord she'd appropriated from one of the drapes in the bedroom. She efficiently secured the woman's hands behind her back, then turned to Alex with a grin. "She must have a glass jaw; she's still out like a light."

Alex was gazing at the woman's unconscious form with dark, mournful eyes. "You shouldn't have done that, Honey," he said sadly.

"But you don't understand, Alex," Honey said briskly, reaching over to pick up a towel from the rack above the tub. She began to dry her legs. Then, as an afterthought, she threw a towel modestly over the redhead's lax, naked body. "She wasn't what she seemed at all. I'm almost sure she's a part of the assassination plot against you and Lance."

"So am I," Alex said gloomily, his eyes still on the redhead. "I suspected it from the first night at the Starburst."

"You suspec—" Honey's lips fell open in surprise. "But why didn't you say anything? Why did you invite her to the Folly?"

"I told you I'd been taught never to trust anyone," he said, his moody glance shifting to Honey's shocked face. "She was a little too eager. When I discovered that she wasn't a real redhead, it was only logical to assume

207

that she was the Judas goat staked out by the hunters." He shrugged, his brawny bronzed shoulders gleaming copper. Abruptly it sank home to Honey that he was totally nude. Thank heavens for those mounds of bubble bath! "I decided I'd rather shift the battleground to my own territory and see if I could lure them into my net."

"Then why did you tell me to leave her alone when I jumped into the tub?" Honey asked, perplexed.

His face darkened in a fierce scowl. "Because it's been two weeks, damn it," he growled. "Why the hell couldn't you have knocked her out *afterward?*"

Honey gazed at him blankly. "Afterward?" Suddenly she started to chuckle, and she sat down on the side of the tub and crossed her legs tailor fashion. Her face was alight with laughter, and her violet eyes danced with impish delight. "Oh, Lord, Alex, I'm sorry. I was afraid she was trying to drown you."

He gave her an indignant glance. "I assure you that no woman living would have tried to murder me at that particular moment."

"I'm sure you're right," she agreed solemnly, her lips quirking. "But surely she's no *great* loss. She wasn't a real redhead anyway."

"She was entirely adequate for the situation," Alex said dryly. "You owe me one, Honey."

"I owe you," she agreed lightly. "There must be a redhead somewhere in the world whom you can trust."

His lips twisted cynically. "I strongly doubt it. But you're the private investigator — you find her for me."

"I just might do that," Honey said thoughtfully.

"I imagine there's some perfectly logical explanation for this scenario," Lance said politely from the doorway. "Would either of you care to enlighten me?" He strolled lazily forward, interestedly eyeing the unconscious woman. "I suppose this is your lethal Delilah, Alex. Very pretty."

"You knew about her too?" Honey asked indignantly. "Why didn't someone tell me? How do you expect me to perform with any sort of efficiency if you both keep me in the dark?"

"You weren't *my* bodyguard, Honey," Alex said, leaning lazily back in the tub. "And Lance was more than satisfied with your performance, I'm sure."

"More than satisfied," Lance agreed solemnly, blue eyes twinkling.

"I guess you know about the launch as well," Honey said, crossly scowling at them both.

"Which one?" Alex asked, one brow arched inquiringly. "Mine or theirs?"

"Which one?" Honey sputtered. "The one in the cove. You mean there are two?"

Lance was squatting down beside Leona Martell now, and he opened her lid to examine judiciously one glassy eye. "Probably not anymore," he said absently. "Alex's men have more than likely dispatched the black hats with their usual efficiency." He looked over at Alex with a frown. "She's really dead to the world, Alex. Did you have to hit her so hard?"

"Don't blame me," Alex disclaimed with a wry grin. "It was your beautiful Amazon, sitting there." He gave Honey an admiring glance. "Dear heaven, but she's got a fantastic right cross."

"Thank you," Honey said automatically, not really hearing them. "Alex's men?"

"Well, Karim's men, actually," Lance said, rising to his feet and strolling around to where Honey was sitting. "Sedikhan Petroleum has its own security force, and he's made sure that they're efficient and deadly. Do you think the old tiger would allow his precious grandson to wander over the face of the earth without making certain that he was well protected?"

"So that was why you refused a bodyguard," Honey said thoughtfully. Then her chin lifted indignantly. "You needed me like you needed a hole in the head!"

Lance kneeled down beside her. "I needed you," he said gently. "I needed you very much." He picked up her right hand and examined it with a frown. "You've bruised your knuckles." He brushed his lips tenderly over the darkening flesh. "You should have been more careful. You didn't have to hit her that hard."

Honey gazed at him with blank disbelief, torn between indignation, a desire to laugh, and that melting tenderness that was so much a part of her love for Lance now. "I'll remember that next time," she said dryly, a tiny smile tugging at her lips.

"I would have liked to see you in action," he said, turning her hand over to kiss the palm lingeringly. "It must have been beautiful. I was right to paint you as a Valkyrie."

"I hate to disturb you, but this bath water is getting cold," Alex said patiently. "I'll give you one minute to get Honey out of here before I get out of this tub." He leered with mock lasciviousness. "Then she'll know what she's missing by settling for a red-haired Scaramouche like you."

Lance stood up and pulled Honey to her feet. "She'd better change out of those wet shorts anyway," he said solicitously. He cast a glance at the still-inert nude redhead. "What are you going to do with her?"

"Nothing, unfortunately," Alex said sadly, then gave Honey a glowering look as she giggled. "I suppose I'll radio the launch and have a dinghy sent ashore to pick her up. They'll all be flown back to Sedikhan to be tried."

They turned to leave, and there was an odd flicker of wistfulness in Alex's dark eyes as he watched Lance's arm slide around Honey's waist with loving familiarity.

"Honey!"

She looked over her shoulder at him inquiringly.

"Remember your promise."

She smiled at him serenely. "I'll remember," she said gently.

"What did you promise him?" Lance asked curiously as he shut the door of their room behind them.

"That's our secret," she tossed teasingly over her shoulder. She was riffling through the drawer of the Korean chest, and drew out a pair of white shorts. "You and Alex have kept enough from me." She frowned with annoyance. "I don't appreciate being treated like an outsider. I'm a qualified professional, damn it. Did it ever occur to you that I might be able to help? I'm not some weak, defenseless, clinging vine, you know."

"Oh, we know, all right," he drawled, his blue eyes twinkling. "Alex is lost in admiration for your dazzling right cross. If I'm not careful, he'll probably try to recruit you for his security force."

"What will happen to that woman and her cohorts?" Honey asked, her face troubled. "I would have thought that they'd be turned over to the State Department rather than the sheik."

"It's better not to ask and better still not to probe," Lance said grimly "Justice can be swift and very ruthless in an absolute monarchy like Sedikhan. Alex is the only human being on the face of the earth whom Karim really cares about. It's not likely that anyone who threatened him would receive any mercy."

"Except you," Honey corrected softly. "He must care a good deal about you, to have been so generous."

Lance shrugged. "Maybe. It's hard to tell with a fierce old buzzard like Karim."

"Yet you're very fond of him," Honey said gently. "It's all there in the portrait you did of him."

"Just because you feel affection for someone is no sign it will be returned, Honey sweet," he said cynically. "I learned that a long time ago." For a moment there was a flicker of melancholy in the sapphire eyes, and then it was gone and he was padding catlike across the room toward her. "Would you like me to help you change?" he asked silkily.

She shook her head firmly. "You know very well where that would lead," she said, trying to frown severely. "And you have my painting to finish. Besides, I have to place a call to Mr. Davies and tell him the latest developments. This will put an end to my assignment for the State Department. You won't need me as your bodyguard now that the danger is past."

"Yes, I will," Lance argued softly as he kissed her lightly on the forehead. "I need you to guard my body from all kinds of dangers." He moved closer, so that her breasts were brushing tantalizingly against his chest. "The danger of cold." He kissed the corner of her lips. "The danger of loneliness." His lips moved to her ear, and he blew in it softly. "The danger of frustration."

His arms went around her, burying his face in her hair. "The portrait will wait, Honey," he said huskily. "Show me how well you can guard me from all those things." His hands were at the fastening of the wet khaki shorts, and somehow she found that she had dropped the white shorts in her hand to the floor.

"I really should call Mr. Davies," she said a trifle breathlessly, for his hands were quickly unbuttoning her white blouse. "This isn't at all professional, Lance."

He unfastened her bra and pushed both the bra and blouse down her arms, until they too fell to the carpet. "Davies will wait, too," he said. "I've never made love to an Amazon," he added thickly. "Is it different from taking my Honey hot to bed?"

She had an idea that he was going to find out very soon. She could never hold out for long when Lance was really bent on seduction . . . not that much seduction was required. As usual, she was feeling as yielding as melting butter as his hands came up to cup her breasts in his warm, hard palms. With thumb and forefinger he plucked at the rosy eager tips until they were hard and thrusting and her breath was coming in little gasps. She closed her eyes, and her hands reached out to clutch him desperately by the shoulders to keep from being swept away into this hot vortex of sensation. "Lance, there are things that we have to discuss," she gasped. He bent his head and brushed his tongue over the nipple he'd aroused to such ardent readiness. "The situation has changed, and I have no valid reason for being here now."

"Nothing could be more valid than this," he said thickly. "Don't talk anymore, sweetheart. I want to love you. Can't you feel how I need you?"

She could indeed, and it filled her with excitement that was slowly turning her own hunger from a flickering flame to a white-hot fire. He was right. Now was not the time for speech, but for that magical ritual that seemed to grow in intensity and beauty every time it was performed.

Her eyes still closed, her hands went up to bury themselves in the thickness of his hair and bring him to her breasts once again. "Then, love me, Lance," she urged huskily, "love me."

EIGHT

"Lance, we've got to talk," Honey said, exasperation sharpening her voice. "You've been putting me off since yesterday morning. I won't stand for it any longer."

Lance finished buttoning his black shirt and looked up with an absent smile. "We'll talk tonight when I come to bed," he said evasively, tucking the shirt into his jeans. "I've got to work now." His eyes twinkled impishly. "I missed an entire day's work, thanks to your insatiable appetite for my virile body, and I've got to make up for it." His gaze moved over her lingeringly. "But you'd better pull that sheet up unless you want me to crawl back into bed and start all over again."

Honey automatically pulled up the sheet and tucked it under her arms, frowning crossly at him. He was being as evasive as a will-o'-the-wisp this morning, and he'd been no better yesterday. Every attempt at speaking seriously to him had been met by diversionary tactics worthy of a five-star general — provided that general had earned those stars in a bordello, she thought ruefully. She'd believed they'd explored every facet of physical love in the past weeks, but Lance had demonstrated last night that they'd just skimmed the surface. And she was wondering just how much of that had been genuine passion.

"Now," she said quietly, a thread of steel in her voice. "Not later. Now, Lance."

He opened his lips to protest, then evidently changed his mind. He smiled at her beguilingly, strolled over to the bed, and sat down beside her. "All right, now," he agreed amiably, taking her hand in both of his. "I'm entirely at your disposal, sweet." He scooted a little closer and bent his head to nibble gently at the soft hollow beneath her collarbone.

Her other hand went automatically up around his neck to curl in the dark flaming hair at the nape of his neck. He was so beautiful, she thought dreamily, the somber black of his shirt only made him look more vibrantly alive than ever. The richness of that molten auburn cap, the sapphire of his eyes, the copper brown of his skin all took on a subtle drama in contrast. His hand reached out and gently tugged the sheet down to her waist, and his lips trailed soft, hot kisses down to the rise of her breasts.

"Lance," she said huskily, her hands tightening around his neck. Then, as he was bearing her back on the bed, she suddenly came to her senses. He was doing it again!

"No, damn it!" she cried, and pushed him away so forcefully that he almost fell off the bed. "No! No! No!" She wound the sheet around her firmly and slid over to the other side of the bed, where she knelt to glare at him belligerently. "We're going to talk!"

His expression was distinctly sulky as he said crossly, "I think you've made yourself clear. I don't know why it won't wait." He scowled. "Say what you have to say and get it over with."

She drew a quick, deep breath. "All right, I will," she said. "I can't stay here any longer. I have to get back to my office. My purpose for being here vanished yesterday, when the threat to your life was lifted."

"That's ridiculous!" he spat explosively. "There's no reason for you to leave. You like it here. We're fantastic together, in bed and out. Why in the hell would you want to go back to Houston? If that Martell woman hadn't been captured, you'd have been content to stay indefinitely."

"But we did catch her, and that's the entire point," Honey argued in exasperation. "I can't just drift along in some fantasy island paradise. I'm not made that way. I have a career and responsibilities."

"You promised to stay with me until after my show," he said stubbornly, his sapphire eyes blazing. "Your precious career can wait until then, can't it? Or isn't it worth it to you anymore?"

"Of course, it's worth it." She sighed wearily. "I fully intend to meet you in New York for the exhibit next month. I'm not trying to break off our affair, Lance. I'll be glad to fly to the island for weekends if you want me to, and perhaps you can come to see me if you're not too busy preparing for your exhibit. It's just that I think it's time to approach our relationship more realistically."

"Sounds charming," Lance said caustically. "Very cool and pragmatic and completely analytic. Exactly what I'd expect from a private investigator. Perhaps you could make up a schedule."

Cool and pragmatic? Every word she was uttering was creating a fresh wound, yet she knew that if she was to keep any part of Lance's respect, she first must respect herself. She'd known since the beginning of

220

their affair that this moment would come.

"If it comes down to it, I just might do that," Honey said coolly. "And I see no harm in being pragmatic. You know as well as I that we can't go on like this forever. We've both got to return to our own lives sometime and go our separate ways."

"It doesn't have to be that way," Lance said haltingly, not looking at her.

"Yes, it does," Honey said softly, her face pale and strained. "I can't give up my work and independence any more than you can. I won't live the life of a mindless parasite even for you, Lance."

His lips twisted bitterly. "You're nothing if not eloquent. You make life with me sound as rewarding as going to the dentist for a root canal."

"Don't be stupid," Honey said impatiently. "You know I find you a very exciting lover. I think that I've made that more than clear. I still want to continue our affair. It just has to be on my terms."

"The hell it does!" Lance said roughly, his face stormy. He jumped to his feet, his eyes blazing down at her. "That cool, anemic little liaison you're describing may be enough for you, but I'll be damned if I'll put up with it. I want more, damn it. And by God, I'll have it!" He turned and strode angrily toward the door.

"Does that mean you want to put an end to our relationship entirely?" she called after him, trying, with that same coolness he'd condemned so passionately, to mask the sick dread she felt.

He turned at the door, his sapphire eyes gleaming like a finely honed blade in his white face. For a moment, the artist and lover she'd grown to know so well was gone and there was once again the shimmer of steel that lay just beneath the surface. "Hell, no," he said softly. "It means that I mean to have it all. I'm not letting you leave me, Honey. It will be a good deal easier on you if you make up your mind to that."

The door closed with a decisive click behind him.

Darn the man, why couldn't he see reason? Didn't he know how it was hurting her to maintain this cool composure when all she wanted to do was throw herself into his arms and do anything he wanted for the rest of her life? Didn't he realize what assuming the role of his mistress in public would do to her? She would grow to hate herself and, worse still, she would grow to hate Lance for what he'd made of her.

There must be some way of convincing him of the validity of her arguments, she thought gloomily, though at the moment she couldn't see it. But there was no question that she must continue to try. She didn't know if she could exist without having at least a small role in Lance's life, and the other option he'd given her was equally unpalatable. There must be a happy medium. She would just have to try again later, after he'd cooled down.

Perhaps she could discuss the problem with Alex and get him to intercede with Lance on her behalf. In the past weeks she'd developed an almost sisterly affection for Ben Raschid, and she knew that he liked her equally. Yes, she would see if Alex could get her viewpoint across to Lance.

With this aim in mind, she threw back the covers and strode swiftly to the bathroom. After brushing her teeth, a quick shower, and a vigorous brushing of her hair until it shone, she emerged twenty minutes later. A swift glance at the clock verified that if she hurried she could still catch Alex at the breakfast table on the terrace. She knew he liked to linger over coffee while he read his correspondence, before officially starting his day. She quickly donned a pair of white jeans, a loose boat-necked scarlet tunic top, and sandals, and ran out of the bedroom and down the stairs.

She might just as well have made a more leisurely toilette, for when she hurried out on the terrace, there was no sign of Alex. The table was set with the usual fastidious elegance, but only for two, and Justine was just setting the customary carafe of hot coffee on the table.

"Mr. Ben Raschid has already finished?" Honey asked disappointedly. She wouldn't dare beard Alex in the library once he'd actually started to work.

Justine shook her head. "He's flown to Houston for the day," she said cheerfully. "He left quite early, and asked me to give you a message." She straightened a bamboo placemat and continued. "He said he'd been on the phone to a Mr. Davies last night and that Mr. Davies was a little put out about the packages being forwarded to Sedikhan instead of to him. He decided to fly over to try to pacify him."

The "packages" being Leona Martell and her criminal accomplices, Honey thought in amusement. She could see how Davies would be a trifle upset at having his authority usurped, but she had no doubt Alex would be able to smooth his ruffled feathers. It didn't make her any happier, however, to have to delay her talk with Alex.

"Will he be coming back this evening?"

she asked as she slipped into her accustomed place at the table.

Justine nodded and picked up the carafe to pour Honey's coffee. "Either tonight or early tomorrow morning. He said he was sure you and Prince Rubinoff could find something to do to amuse yourselves." The last sentence was stated impassively, but Honey could almost see the mocking gleam in Alex's dark eyes as he was giving the housekeeper the message. "Will Prince Rubinoff be joining you for breakfast?"

"No, I'm sure he's gone to the studio to work, Justine," Honey said quietly. "You might take him some coffee right now and sandwiches later for lunch. He'll probably be working all day."

Justine nodded again and quietly disappeared into the house, leaving Honey sitting morosely, gazing blindly out at the stunningly lovely seascape view from the terrace.

She finished her coffee and tried to eat a little but finally ended by pushing her plate away distastefully. Perhaps she'd go down to the beach and try to while away a few hours. It would be useless to try to read in such a tense state.

It was while she was striding down the path to the beach that she first heard the now-familiar throbbing sound of helicopter rotors, and she stopped in surprise. Her first thought was that it might be Alex returning, but she dismissed that idea as soon as it occurred to her. Alex couldn't have possibly completed his task and come back already.

She shaded her eyes and soon determined that it wasn't the orange helicopter that she'd become accustomed to seeing on the landing pad at the foot of the hill, but a brilliant blue-and-white one. Yet there was no question that its destination was the Folly. Her eyes narrowed curiously on the aircraft as it descended toward the landing pad like an ungainly butterfly. Then she accelerated her steps and strode hurriedly down the hill toward the pad.

When she arrived, it was to see a khaki-clad, gray-haired man, with "Sunbelt Helicopter Service" imprinted on the back of his shirt, assisting a dark-haired woman in a lovely melon pants suit out of the helicopter.

The woman looked up as Honey appeared beside them, and gave her an incisive glance. "Ach, no wonder," she boomed cheerfully. "You're even more attractive than your picture, Honey Winston." She smiled with sunny friendliness. "Permit me to introduce myself. I'm the Baroness Bettina von Feltenstein. Now, tell me, where are Alex and Lance hiding? They can't have been so cowardly as to send you out to face me alone."

Bettina von Feltenstein? This was the Teutonic Terror of Alex's description? This woman was so far removed from Honey's mental image that she could feel her lips drop open in surprise. Where was the sleek, beautiful vamp of her imaginings? There was nothing in the least sleek about the woman facing her. If her carriage had not been so graceful, her small, plump figure might even have been considered dumpy. And she certainly could not be termed beautiful, though her glowing complexion was really magnificent, and the large, luminous brown eyes behind the stylish tortoiseshell glasses were snapping with vitality.

"I'm not what you expected either," the baroness guessed shrewdly, her eyes narrowing on Honey's surprised face. "I wonder just what they told you about me." She shrugged and grinned with gamine charm, her brown eyes twinkling. "Nothing very complimentary, I'm sure."

"Nothing very much, Baroness," Honey recovered enough to say. "They only mentioned you in passing."

"Really? I'm disappointed that my phone calls had so little impact." She made a wry face. "But then, that's why I'm here. I hate telephones. It's so easy for people to be conveniently disconnected."

Honey smothered a smile and tried to reply with appropriate solemnity. "It certainly is. I'm sorry that you didn't let Alex know you were coming, however. He left for Houston this morning and may not be back until tomorrow."

"I doubt if he'd have changed his plans," the baroness said dryly. "In fact, he might have accelerated them. Alex and I aren't exactly soulmates. Lance is still here, of course." It was a statement, not a question.

Honey nodded, feeling a trifle bemused. It was impossible not to like the baroness, despite her blatant aggressiveness. "Yes, he's still here, but he's in his studio working. Would you like me to take you to him?"

"Not at the moment," the baroness said. "It's really you I came to see anyway." She turned to the helicopter pilot and instructed briskly, "You will wait here, yes? We will be back shortly." She didn't wait for the man's casual nod before turning back to Honey and slinging her large Gucci bag over her shoulder. "Now, where can we go so that we won't be disturbed?"

"I suppose we could go for a walk on the beach," Honey said slowly. She had heard the woman's name only in casual conversation, and she was sure Alex hadn't mentioned that she'd be coming to the island. Why would the baroness fly thousands of miles just to see her?

"That will be fine," Bettina von Feltenstein said. She looked down wryly at her exquisitely crafted high heels. "I guess I should have expected to run into this on an island." She calmly took off the shoes and slipped them into her voluminous shoulder bag. "It's fortunate that I always carry an extra pair of hose. These will be shredded to pieces by the time we get back." She gestured to Honey to precede her. "Lead on, Miss Winston. I'll try to keep up with those long, lovely legs of yours." Her lips turned down gloomily. "You would have to be tall as well as gorgeous."

Honey gave her a questioning glance before obediently leading the way down the palm-bordered path to the beach. The German woman didn't speak again until they reached the lower reaches of the hill and the trail widened enough for her to come alongside.

"You even carry yourself well," the baroness said moodily. "You'd be surprised at

how many tall women have an absolutely
atrocious posture. Do you know how many
years I've studied ballet to get a slight edge
over you sultry giantesses? Did you ever
study ballet, Miss Winston?"

Honey shook her head, thinking of her
very spartan upbringing in the orphanage.
"I'm afraid not, Baroness," she replied gently.

"I suspected that," she said mournfully.
"There's no justice in the world." She
peered owlishly up at Honey through the
thick lenses of her horn-rimmed glasses.
"You're even younger than I am."

"Not very much," Honey said soothingly.
How on earth had she been put in the position of comforting this small, strange rival
for Lance's affections? "I'm twenty-four,
Baroness."

"And I'm thirty-one," Bettina von Feltenstein said tersely. "I'm one year older than
Lance. And call me Bettina; I will find it
very hard to speak with frankness if we're
formal." She added, "I will call you Honey.
What an abominable name. Why do you not
change it?"

She hadn't noticed that the baroness was
shy about speaking her mind, Honey
thought in amusement. "I agree with you,
but it's not worth the bother," she said

lightly. "How did you know I was here, Bar— Bettina?"

"Can we sit down?" Bettina asked abruptly, halting in her tracks. "This hot sand is most uncomfortable on my feet." Without waiting for Honey to agree, she plopped herself down on the sand in the shade of a palm tree. "I saw your picture in the newspaper and I thought it worthwhile to find out all I could about you," she said grimly. "Actually, the expression on Lance's face told me quite a bit."

"Newspaper?" Honey asked, dropping down beside her. Her brow creased in puzzlement. Then she remembered the photographer in the lobby of the hotel the night before they'd left. It seemed very far removed from her present existence. "They used that picture of Lance and me?"

The baroness opened her large shoulder bag and drew out a folded newspaper.

"They used it," she said curtly. "Complete with smutty innuendoes and juicy references to Lance's very disreputable past. Lance's parents were very displeased when they called me after they'd seen it."

"You know Lance's parents?" Honey asked absently as she spread out the newspaper. She glanced only briefly at her own shocked face as she stood in the curve of

231

Lance's arm. It was the expression on Lance's face that caught her attention. He was looking down at her with desire and tenderness and a fierce protectiveness that filled her with a quiet joy.

"Our families have been very close since we were small children," Bettina said softly. "When Lance wasn't in Sedikhan, we were practically inseparable. Their Majesties have always approved of a match between us."

"So I understand," Honey said quietly, carefully refolding the newspaper and handing it back. "Yet the marriage has never come to pass."

"It will in time," Bettina said with complete confidence. "I'm a very determined woman, Honey. This marriage is not only desirable, but it's necessary for Lance."

"To keep the royal bloodlines pure and unpolluted?" Honey asked tartly, unconsciously moistening her lips. The absolute certainty that the woman exuded was making her uneasy despite the comforting message generated by Lance's expression in the newspaper photo.

"No, of course not," the baroness said. "I have a great respect for selective breeding, but there have been too many dynamic leaders born on the wrong side of the blanket for me to be a complete fanatic on the subject. I only use that argument with Lance because I can't tell him the truth."

"The truth?" Honey asked slowly.

"I love him," Bettina said simply, with utter sincerity. "I've loved him all my life. Everything I've studied and worked for since childhood has been to prepare me to be a fitting wife for him." Her face was earnest. "I'll be everything that he could ask for in a mate, Honey."

"Why are you telling me this?" Honey asked, looking away from that earnest little face to stare blindly out at the gentle roll of the surf. Suddenly she was no longer finding the situation amusing. It hurt to think of Lance in the intimacy of marriage with any woman. "Your relationship with Lance is none of my business."

"I don't usually go around confiding my most intimate feelings to strangers," Bettina said bluntly. "This is the first time I've felt it necessary to approach one of Lance's *petites amies.* After I saw that picture, I thought we'd better meet. I was frightened. I'd never seen Lance look at any woman like that before. I wanted to come to an understanding with you before a terrible mistake was made."

"Should I be honored that you consider me a threat?" Honey asked tightly. "I'm sorry if I can't see that we have anything to talk about. We obviously play two very different roles in Lance's life. There's no reason why the two should encroach upon each other."

"Ah, you realize that?" Bettina asked with a relieved sigh. "That is good. I was afraid that you might have hopes for a more permanent place in his affections. That is, of course, totally impossible."

Honey flinched at the sudden thrust of pain that struck her. "Of course," she said huskily.

The baroness's eyes were warmly sympathetic as she reached over and gave Honey's hand a bracing squeeze. "None of us can have everything," she said gently. "We must all compromise."

"And what have you given up, Baroness?" Honey asked sharply, blinking back the tears and turning to her with her chin lifted in defiance. "What do you intend to compromise?"

"I've given up the hope of ever having Lance look at me as he did at you in that newspaper photograph," she answered quietly, and the pain in her face mirrored that in Honey's. "I know that he'll never love me or desire me as he does you. I've had to accept that."

"How can you?" Honey broke out fiercely. "How can you possibly want a man who doesn't want you?"

"Because he'll learn to care for me," Bettina said serenely. "There are many ways of caring. If I cannot have his passion, I will earn his trust, his gratitude, even his affection." Her smile was bittersweet. "It's not everything, but it will be enough."

She would not feel sorry for the woman, Honey thought feverishly. This strange empathy that existed between them was far more dangerous than if the baroness had been openly antagonistic. How much more difficult it was to fight against a rival who loved Lance as much as she did.

"Is that what you came to tell me? That I have no real place in Lance's life?" Honey asked bitterly.

Bettina shook her head. "No, that isn't why I came," she said gently. "I came to tell you that there is room for both of us. I am a modern woman, and I have come to terms with the knowledge that you give Lance something that I can't." She shrugged wearily. "Glamour, sex, the love mystique — I don't know. Whatever it is, he doesn't see it in me. You'll have to supply it." She looked away. "I want you to know that as long as the two of you are discreet, I will ignore your relationship regardless of how long it continues."

"That's very generous of you," Honey said slowly, and there was no sarcasm in her voice. In the baroness's place, she doubted very much if she could have made a similar offer.

"Not really," Bettina said throatily. "As I said, I made it my business to find out a great deal about you, Honey Winston. If you and Lance are lovers, it is because you have a genuine affection for him. That is essential." She looked up fiercely. "For, whatever happens, he must not be hurt. You understand that?"

"I understand," Honey said huskily. "I love him very much too, you know."

"I don't know," Bettina said quietly. "But I'm about to find out. How generous is your love, Honey?"

"I don't know what you mean."

"I want you to leave Lance," Bettina said, but then held up her hand at Honey's cry of protest. "Not permanently. Haven't I just told you that I don't expect that? Just until after Lance's exhibit in New York next month."

"You know about that?" Honey asked faintly.

"Alex told me on the phone the other

evening," she said wryly. "I think he was trying to put me off by extending the hope that I'd see Lance in New York. I knew as soon as I heard about it that it might be the answer to all Lance's problems with his parents." She smiled sadly. "Do you know I've only seen that one portrait in the library? Do you know how envious I am that it is you who has seen all his work and persuaded him to show it?"

"What problems with his parents?" Honey asked curtly. This was getting more painful by the moment. "It's my understanding that they were never close."

"Lance has always wanted his parents' respect and admiration. This exhibit could give him that," Bettina said quietly. "I want to try to persuade them to attend the exhibit and encourage a reconciliation. There's only one difficulty."

"Me," Honey said huskily, her throat tight and aching with pain.

Bettina nodded. "If your liaison continues, it's bound to attract publicity." Her lips twisted ruefully. "Lance always does. Needless to say, we don't need to upset his parents while I'm trying to negotiate a truce." Her brown eyes were sober. "Do you love Lance enough to put his welfare above your own, Honey? It will be for only a little over a month, and then you can resume your relationship."

"You don't want me to see Lance at all?" Honey asked. And she'd thought becoming only a weekend lover was going to be difficult. She felt a shiver of loneliness run through her.

"You know that wouldn't be wise," Bettina said softly, her face sympathetic. "It would be impossible to keep your association quiet, after that newspaper story. If you're going to do something, do it right."

"I'm afraid I don't have your innate incisiveness," Honey said, her voice shaking despite her effort to steady it. "I don't know if I can do it."

"Of course you can," Bettina said briskly. "I'll make it as easy on you as I can. I'll fly you back to Houston this morning in the helicopter. Then I'll come back and explain everything to Lance. You won't even have to speak to him yourself. I think you would find that very difficult. Yes?"

"Impossible," Honey agreed miserably. "You have it all planned."

"My incisiveness is generally accompanied by my efficiency," Bettina said, her brown eyes twinkling. "You can phone him from Houston, if you feel it's necessary." She made a face. "I wouldn't recommend it.

Very frustrating things, telephones."

Honey ran her hand distractedly through her hair. "I don't know. It's all coming too fast. I've got to think."

"Of course you do," the baroness agreed promptly. "I have no intention of rushing you into a decision you'll regret later." She stood up and meticulously brushed the powdery sand from the melon pants suit. "I'll go back to the helicopter and wait for you there. You're a very loving, intelligent woman. I'm sure you'll make the right choice." She padded away, her plump figure indomitably majestic despite her stockinged feet and the little hops she occasionally gave to avoid the heat of the noonday sand.

Indomitable. That was the right word for her, Honey thought. She had swept boldly into her life, and suddenly everything was colored by the baroness's viewpoint. It was hard to ignore anyone as clear-thinking and fiercely loving as Bettina had proven to be. She had known Lance and his family for years, and that made her a far better judge than Honey as to what was best for Lance.

She frowned as the thought occurred to her that she would be making it ridiculously easy for a rival as strong as Bettina by removing herself from the picture for over a month. Was that what the baroness had in mind? Somehow she didn't think so. There had been too much sincerity in Bettina's face. Too much pain. Besides, if the relationship that existed between Lance and her would not withstand a month's separation, then it deserved to be severed. There were so many problems already surfacing in their affair that must be solved if they were to continue with any kind of harmony. Perhaps a month's hiatus would permit them time to think and see each other's point of view a little more clearly.

Why was she sitting here, when she knew her decision was really already made? She'd known when Bettina threw out the challenge to her love for Lance that she would have to pick up the gauntlet. She got to her feet and automatically dusted herself off as she set off toward the path that led to the landing pad.

Bettina was leaning against the helicopter, and she straightened slowly, her face tense as Honey appeared beside her.

"I'm going with you," Honey said curtly. "But it's got to be now. I don't want to see Lance before I go." Otherwise she would never have the courage to leave him. The pain was already shooting through her.

"Very wise," Bettina said, nodding. "You don't want to pack a bag?"

Honey shook her head. "Alex can have Justine pack my things and send them on to me. I don't want to go back to the house."

"Then we'll go," Bettina said briskly, opening the helicopter door. Following Honey into the aircraft, she gave the pilot a curt command and settled back into her seat. "Fasten your seatbelt," she ordered, adjusting her own.

Honey automatically obeyed, and they were soon spiraling into the heavens before leveling out and initiating a course eastward. She couldn't resist a look back at the emerald dot in the sapphire sea. It was a mistake, for she soon found the brilliant colors running together as the tears welled up in her eyes.

Bettina was watching her sympathetically. "You're doing the right thing, you know," she said gently. "That should help a little."

"Should it?" Honey said huskily. "Then there's something wrong. I don't think it does." She turned for one last look at Londale's Folly, but she was too late. It had already disappeared from view.

NINE

"Frankly, I think you're out of your mind," Nancy said bluntly, leaning back in her chair and regarding Honey, sitting in the visitor's chair by the desk. "You admit you're absolutely mad about the man, yet you're fading out of the picture for an entire month?" Her lips curved cynically. "Contrary to what you may have heard, absence does not make the heart grow fonder. Particularly when a man has as many women throwing themselves at him as your Prince Charming."

Honey flinched. That thought had been plaguing her ever since she had made the decision. It had been only a matter of hours, and she was already having doubts — not about the essential rightness of Bettina's arguments. Lance must have this chance for a reconciliation with his parents. Families were important, and who should know better than she, who had never had one? She wouldn't let Lance continue to be an emotional orphan, cut off from his parents and brother, not if there was any way that she could prevent it.

Yet she couldn't deny that it was frightening to face the ramifications of her actions. While Nancy's comment might have been tainted with the bitterness of her broken marriage, there was no question but that Honey was taking an enormous risk.

There had been no words of commitment spoken between them in all that golden halcyon period at the island. There had been words of passion. There had been laughter. There had been moments of tender exploration of the mind and emotions. That had seemed enough at the time. It was almost as if they'd both been afraid to disturb their magical Brigadoon with thoughts of the outside world. Once Lance was back in the reality of his own world, would that magic still hold?

"Then, I'd better find that out now, hadn't I?" Honey asked lightly, smiling with no little effort. "I know that I'm not going to change, and I don't think I'm equipped to handle a one-sided affair."

"You're not equipped to handle an affair, period. Why couldn't you have started out in the minor leagues and worked your way up to the big boys?" Nancy threw up her hands expressively. "Oh, no, your first affair has to be with Lusty Lance. Then you have to go and fall in love with him! Why couldn't you have chosen a nice, tame stockbroker or a used-car salesman?"

"I guess I just don't have your good taste," Honey said, her lips quirking despite the heaviness of her spirit. "I find I have a distinct partiality for princes."

"Thank goodness there aren't that many around," Nancy said gloomily. "For God's sake, stay away from Italy. I understand that they pop out from under every bush over there."

"I'll keep that in mind," Honey promised solemnly, her violet eyes twinkling. "What is the state of our finances?"

"Better than usual, thanks to Señora Gomez's fee and the check we received last week from the State Department from Mr. Davies," Nancy replied. "Why?"

"I'm going away for a week or two," Honey said. "I just wanted to make sure that there was enough in the coffers to pay your salary and the bills until I get back."

"Am I allowed to ask where you're going?" Nancy asked caustically. "You're getting to be an absentee employer. The mailman will wonder if I'm just making you up, like that private detective on television."

"I don't think that would be a very good idea," Honey said quietly. "If you don't know where I am, you can't be coerced into telling anyone. The baroness has arranged for a place where I can stay for a bit, until Lance gets discouraged looking for me. I'll call you every few days to check in and make sure everything is running smoothly."

"Leaving me to fight off the ravening hordes." Nancy sighed. "You're probably right not to tell me where you're going. I could withstand bulldozing tactics, but if your Lance decides to use that notorious charm on me, I'd be sunk. I'd probably melt like an iceberg in Death Valley."

Honey couldn't have agreed more. Hadn't she found that charisma well-nigh irresistible from the moment they'd met? But she wouldn't think of that; it only made what she was doing that much harder. "I'm sure you'll survive," she said. "I'll call the day after tomorrow, when I've settled in."

Three hours later she'd finished packing her suitcases and was checking the tiny kitchen in her efficiency apartment to make sure that the utilities were turned off. There was nothing in the refrigerator to spoil, and there was nothing left to do but write a note to the manager of the apartment explaining her absence. She had just completed that when the phone rang.

"He just called, Honey," Nancy burst out as soon as she picked up the receiver. "I told him you'd already left town, but I don't think he believed me. I think you're probably going to have a visitor in the next hour or two."

"Do you know where he was calling from?" Honey asked, biting her lip worriedly. She knew very well that if she had to face Lance, her resolution, which was shaky at best, would vanish in the first strong breeze. And that seductive charm of Lance's could escalate to hurricane force when he chose. Which was the reason she'd opted not to face him in the first place.

"From the island," Nancy replied, to her intense relief. "But you can bet he won't be staying there."

"I'll be gone by the time he gets to Houston, then," Honey said. "Thanks for the warning, Nancy." She quietly replaced the receiver.

She hesitated a moment and then picked up the receiver and placed a call to the island, person-to-person to Alex Ben Raschid.

"Hello." Alex's voice was curt with impatience when he came on the line, and became even more so when she identified herself. "Damn it Honey, do you know what hell you've raised? Why the devil did you leave the Folly without speaking to Lance first? He's been tearing around here like a madman ever since Bettina got back from practically kidnapping you."

"Is he still there, Alex?" Honey asked, when she could get a word in edgewise.

"He took off in the helicopter as soon as he finished talking to your secretary. For God's sake, how could you pull a stunt like this? When I got back to the island, I found Lance in a positive fury, the Teutonic Terror sobbing heartbrokenly, and you vanished from the face of the earth." Alex's voice was sharp with exasperation. "I'd just spent a whole bloody trying day convincing Davies that my grandfather wasn't going to take the entire assassination team out and behead them, and I come back to this!"

"I'm sorry, Alex," Honey said contritely. "I never meant to be a problem to you." Then she asked curiously, "Do they really behead people in Sedikhan?"

"Very rarely," Alex answered absently. "Honey, whatever possessed you to let Bettina bulldoze you into leaving? I thought you had more backbone than to let her intimidate you."

"It wasn't like that, Alex," Honey said. "It was my decision."

"You'll forgive me if I doubt that," Alex said dryly. "I'm familiar with Bettina's determination."

"So am I, now," Honey said ruefully. "But she wouldn't have been able to convince me to do something I wasn't willing to do. I'm not so easily swayed, Alex."

"I didn't think so until tonight," Alex said slowly. "Why did you do it, Honey? Lance was almost a raving lunatic. I've never seen him act like that before."

Honey ignored the question. "I want you to give him a message for me, Alex," Honey said quietly. "Will you please tell him I'll get in touch with him in six weeks' time? That is, if he still wants me to."

"If he still wan—" Alex echoed incredulously. "You're going to stretch this madness out for another six weeks? Good God, he'll tear Houston apart to find you."

"It won't do him any good. I'm leaving town tonight," she said gently. "Please just give him the message. Thank you for everything, Alex. You're a good friend."

There was a short silence. "You're making a mistake, Honey," Alex said quietly. "Lance isn't going to sit with folded hands, tamely waiting for you to get in touch with him."

When she didn't answer, he continued with even greater deliberation. "And I hope I am your friend, Honey. I like you better than any woman I've ever known. But Lance is almost a brother to me. If it comes to a choice, then I'll have to side with him."

"I understand that," Honey replied. "But it won't come down to choices. I hope that I'll see you in six weeks, too. Good-bye, Alex."

"I rather think it will be a great deal sooner than that," Alex said softly. "Good-bye, Honey." The connection was broken with a decisive click.

Honey replaced the receiver, an uneasy frown wrinkling her brow. That last rejoinder had an oddly ominous overtone. Then she determinedly shrugged it off. It must be her imagination. Alex might be intimidating to his business rivals and political enemies, but he was her friend. It was foolish to be afraid.

Yet for some reason her final preparations for departure were even more hurried than was actually necessary. Fifteen minutes later she flicked out the lights, locked the door, and carried her suitcase down the wrought-iron stairs to her ancient blue Nova.

"I've saddled up Missy for you, Miss Winston," Hank called with a friendly grin that caused the sun creases to deepen about his keen gray eyes. "I hope that's all right."

"Missy will be fine, Hank," Honey answered with a smile. There hadn't really been any choice, Honey thought wryly as the stable-hand gave her a leg up into the saddle. Missy was as gentle as a rocking horse and the only animal in the entire remuda of horses on the Circle D Dude Ranch that she could manage to stay on. Horseback riding had definitely not been considered a necessary asset at the orphanage, and Honey had discovered as a beginner that she had little or no aptitude for equestrian pursuits. In the week she'd been here, she'd only managed to learn the bare rudiments, and wasn't at all sure that the aching muscles and decidedly tender derriere were worth the bother.

Yet she had to admit that these solitary morning rides did have their pleasant aspects. It was a relief not to have to maintain a sociable facade in front of the other guests, and she was so inept a rider that she had to concentrate to keep even Missy under control. It was virtually the only time she could shake the gloom and apathy that had beset her since she'd left the island.

Twenty minutes later she reined in at the little pine-shaded oblong lake, as was her custom, and slid gratefully from the saddle. She rubbed her jean-clad derriere ruefully, wondering if she'd ever learn not to bounce when that dratted horse decided to trot. After carefully putting the reins over the mare's head, as she'd been taught, she strolled down to the water's edge. This was her favorite spot on the entire ranch. Its quiet, serene beauty was a soothing balm to her troubled spirit, a balm that she dearly needed.

She leaned against the rough, gnarled bark of a pine and wearily closed her eyes, lifting her face in sensual contentment to the warm kiss of the sun. She supposed she should have been grateful to Bettina for arranging such luxurious accommodations at this isolated dude ranch, a short distance west of Houston. It was not the baroness's fault that she was a city girl and found all these trail rides and bucolic shenanigans a little wearing on the nerves. She'd be glad when she could go back to Houston and get to work again.

That might not be as soon as she hoped. When she'd called Nancy yesterday, it was to be told that Lance had not abandoned his search for her and was driving Nancy crazy with phone calls and general harassment. Nancy had sounded frazzled and very cross. Evidently Lance was being quite unpleasant to the poor woman.

"Miss Winston?" the voice was deep, masculine, and very respectful.

Honey's lids flew open, to see two young men, dressed impeccably in dark business suits and discreetly patterned ties.

She hadn't heard them approach, yet they were standing only a few feet from her. They must have moved very quietly. "Yes, I'm Miss Winston," she answered.

"We've been looking for you, Miss Winston," the sandy-haired man said almost reproachfully. "We'd like you to come with us, please."

"Looking for me?" Honey asked, puzzled. "Are you from the ranch?" She knew before he shook his head that they were not. Those suits were far too expensive and cosmopolitan.

"No, ma'am, we're not," the dark-skinned man said gently. "We have our car parked about a quarter of a mile down the road. I wonder if we could persuade you to go with us now? We really do have to be on our way."

Honey shook her head as if to clear it. This was bizarre. "Why should I go anywhere with you? I don't even know you, and I certainly don't intend to get in any car with you."

"I'm sorry. We didn't introduce ourselves, did we?" the sandy-haired man asked with a frown. "I'm John Sax, and my friend, here, is Hassan Khalin. We're both employees of Alex Ben Raschid. We've been sent to fetch you."

"Fetch me?" Honey asked blankly. Employees of Alex Ben Raschid? Then she suddenly realized just exactly what manner of employees Alex had sent to find her. These soft-voiced young men must be members of that lethal security force Lance had mentioned. Now that she'd examined them more closely, she could detect that dangerous coiled tension beneath the smooth exterior that was the trademark of the professional. She stiffened and straightened slowly, her muscles tightening instinctively. "Then I'm afraid you've made a wasted journey," she said quietly, "for I have no intention of coming with you."

John Sax frowned in genuine concern. "Please don't take that attitude, Miss Winston," he pleaded, his blue eyes troubled. "You really must come with us. We have our orders."

She was tempted to tell them what they could do with their orders. How dare Alex do this to her? It was practically barbaric.

"Too bad," she said between her teeth.

"Then you'll have to go back to your employer and tell him that I refuse to accommodate him. Good-bye, gentlemen."

"But we can't do that," Hassan Khalin protested. "We do have our instructions, as John said, Miss Winston. We must take you with us or be in quite a bit of trouble with Ben Raschid ourselves." He shook his head. "It's not very comfortable to be in that position, Miss Winston. Won't you change your mind?"

"No," Honey said emphatically, her face clouding. "If you want me to come with you, you'll have to use force."

The two men exchanged resigned glances. "We have a problem there as well, you see," John Sax admitted gloomily. "Ben Raschid said that he'd take us apart if we so much as disturbed a hair on your head. It's not the easiest assignment we've been given."

Well, at least Alex had had the courtesy to include that gracious little addition to his instructions. "You do have a problem," she said gently, her eyes narrowing. "For I don't intend to go peacefully, and that means not only a displaced coiffure but bruises and perhaps even cuts and scratches." She lifted a brow. "And while you're handling me with kid gloves, I can assure you that I'm not going to be equally kind. I'll be inflicting as much damage as I possibly can." Her gleaming smile had a touch of the tiger. "I think you'll be surprised at how much mayhem that constitutes, gentlemen."

"So we understand, Miss Winston," John Sax said with a gleam of genuine admiration in his bright blue eyes. "We were given an extensive dossier on you. Your credentials are very impressive, as was Ben Raschid's description of your prowess." He sighed. "Yes, the situation is very complicated."

"Then don't you think it would be better to give up and run back to your employer?" Honey suggested silkily. "Tell him that if he wants to speak to me, he can come and see me himself." And by that time, with any luck, she would be far away from the Circle D.

The same thought evidently had occurred to Sax, for he was shaking his head with a reproving grin. "You know we can't do that, Miss Winston," he said quietly. "Nice try, though."

"Then I don't know what you're going to do," Honey said flatly. "We seem to be at an impasse."

Khalin's face was gloomy. "We were afraid that just such a situation would occur, weren't we, John?"

His cohort nodded, an equally unhappy

expression on his face. "We discussed the problem in some depth, and we could come to only one solution."

This was taking on all the nuances of a farce. It seemed impossible that she was standing here in this lovely sylvan setting talking so calmly to these soft-voiced, dangerous young men.

"And that is?" she asked warily.

She'd thought she was prepared, but when they moved toward her, it was with such deadly swiftness and smoothly coordinated timing that it caught her off guard. Khalin feinted to the left to distract her attention, and Sax followed through to her right. She only had time for a karate chop to Khalin's throat, which connected with a very satisfying thunk, before she felt a tiny sting on her arm, like the bite of a mosquito.

Then she was watching Khalin stumble to his knees with an out-of-sync deliberateness that was like slow motion. Everything was suddenly dimming, and she felt an instant of panic. Then she felt nothing at all.

Ten

When Honey awoke, she had that same heavy, distorted feeling, as if she were a swimmer fighting her way to the surface from the ocean's depths. Yet when she opened her eyes, it was with a sense of dreamy euphoria, rather than with the headache and nausea that she would have expected of a drug-induced unconsciousness.

Her gaze traveled around the room, and what she saw convinced her that she was still in a dream state. There couldn't be a room like this outside of a Turkish harem. She seemed to be reclining on a heap of tasseled white satin pillows. A gorgeous Persian carpet in delicate shades of pale blue and spring green on a cream background covered a polished parquet floor. There was even a copper brazier filled with glowing coals on the low teak table next to her that was giving off a heady, spicy fragrance. Incense? Yes, she was sure it was incense, she thought dreamily. It fit in perfectly with the rest of the fantasy.

She looked down at her own apparel and was not at all surprised to find herself garbed in sheer chiffon amethyst harem pants, her silken stomach quite bare and the thrusting fullness of her breasts swathed in a matching pearl-trimmed top. What else would she be wearing in an Arabian Nights fantasy?

She turned on her side, waiting for the dream to fade and go away, and her gaze fell on a piece of folded notepaper on the table. She reached out a lazy hand and took it from the table, unfolding it with idle curiosity.

The words jumped out at her, shocking her into wakefulness.

Sorry, Honey. I did warn you.

Alex

Honey sat bolt upright on the silken cushions, her violet eyes blazing with fury. What kind of wild practical joke was this? The kidnapping was obviously Alex's doing, but this mad harem charade was completely at odds with everything she knew of him.

"Ah, you're awake at last."

Honey looked up, her heart leaping with joy and her face alight. It clouded swiftly as she gazed with rapidly returning fury at Lance, standing in the doorway. No one could argue about the dashing figure he made as he stood there, dressed in khaki riding pants tucked into mirror-bright black boots and a white shirt worn unbuttoned almost to the waist. My God, he was even wearing a white headdress!

Honey jumped off the cushions and struggled to her feet. "What the devil is going on here?" she shouted, facing him belligerently across the room.

Lance placed both hands on his hips, his face taking on a demonic leer. "Are you not woman enough to know?" he asked hoarsely.

"For God's sake, have you gone absolutely bananas?" Honey asked, running her hand through her hair distractedly. "They could put you away for a stunt like this. Have you completely lost touch with reality?"

Lance dropped the melodramatic pose, his face turning grim. "Hell, no," he said, his hands falling to his sides. "I just thought that you'd like to enjoy for one last time the pleasures of never-never land. Isn't that what you want from me? A romantic weekend affair with Lusty Lance, with no commitments or permanent ties? You couldn't wait to get off the island once your precious job was done, could you?" He tore the headdress off and threw it violently aside. "Well, the romantic fantasy's over. We're living in the real world now, Honey, and it's time you faced up to it. I'm not letting you run away again."

Honey's lips were slightly parted. "I didn't run away from the island," she protested. "I had a perfectly good reason for —"

"Bull!" Lance said succinctly, walking toward her with swift, pantherish strides. "Even you couldn't be so naive as to believe that story Bettina laid on you. Hell, yes, I was cut up, as a kid, when I couldn't seem to do anything right as far as my family was concerned; but, like all kids, I adjusted pretty damn quick. I'm certainly not pining for a reunion, as Bettina seems to think. No, that wasn't why you were so eager to leave. It was just an excuse. You were scared to death I was going to ask for something you weren't ready to give."

Was he right? Had she really been so eager to believe Bettina's interpretation of Lance's feelings because she was afraid of the eventual pain that would attend any long-term affair with him?

"I see you're not denying it," Lance said tightly. He stopped before her, his face taut

260

and pale beneath his tan. "Well, I'm going to ask it of you anyway. I'm gambling that you care more for me than you do for that blasted career of yours. You're going to marry me, Honey."

"What!" Honey's eyes widened in stunned surprise.

"There's no use you arguing about it," Lance said roughly. "I'm not about to let you leave me again until the knot is well and truly tied." His hands grasped her shoulders, and he was looking down into her face with an intensity that made her breath catch in her throat. "Think about it, Honey," he urged persuasively. "Would you have risked your life saving those blasted paintings if I wasn't more to you than just your first lover? We've got everything going for us. Sex, companionship, love." Then, as she would have spoken, he held up his hand. "Yes, *love,* damn it! You do love me, even if you won't admit it. Would it be so much of a sacrifice to give up your work and marry me?"

"I can't do that," Honey said dazedly, feeling as if she were going mad. "My work? What about you? You're a prince, for heaven's sake."

"That's not my profession, that's an accident of birth," he said indignantly. "I'm

261

an artist. You may be contemptuous of princes, but I know damn well you like my alter ego."

"I'm not contemptuous . . ." She trailed off helplessly. Then she tried again. "Royal princes don't marry orphanage brats like me. I don't even know who my father was." She shook her head. "I never expected you to want to marry me."

"Humility in a Valkyrie is definitely not becoming," Lance said with a flicker of amusement in his face. "Why shouldn't I want to marry you? You're the other half of me."

"I'm not humble," Honey said indignantly. "I know very well that any man would be lucky to marry a woman with my assets. I'm intelligent, hardworking, reasonably attractive, I have a fairly good sense of humor, I —"

Lance stopped her with his lips on hers, and when he lifted his head, he said tenderly, "You don't have to list your qualifications, love. You've already got the job." He shook his head ruefully. "That is, if you think you can put up with this slightly mad artist for the next fifty years or so. Lord knows why you would want to, after what you've been exposed to in the past few weeks. Attempted assassination, tropical storms, interfering baronesses, as well as my own blasted neglect and self-absorption. I can't even promise you that our future together won't be more of the same." His expression was grave and heart-catchingly tender. "I can only promise that you'll have all of my love for the rest of my days. Is that enough?"

"Oh, yes, that's enough," Honey answered, her throat aching with emotion. She buried her face in his shoulder. "Oh, Lance, I love you so much. I wasn't sure if I could bear it if it wasn't going to be forever for you, too."

"What a silly woman you are, Honey sweet," he said softly. "You were the one who was always talking about our affair as if it were going to end tomorrow. I always knew exactly what I wanted." He was stroking her hair with a gentle hand. "My Honey's head always on the next pillow and her hand in mine on every road I travel."

The words were as touchingly solemn as a wedding vow, and Honey drew a deep, quivering breath at the brilliant flame of happiness that exploded within her. "Your hand in mine on every road and byway," Honey repeated huskily, and that, too, was a promise. She looked up, her violet eyes star bright. "Forever."

Lance's face was so beautifully tender that

Honey felt her heart melt with answering love for him. "It's crazy," she protested weakly. "For God's sake, I'd be Princess Honey. Did you ever hear anything so ridiculous?"

"I like it," Lance said tenderly, his sapphire eyes twinkling. "And you'd be a honey of a princess."

She groaned, her lips twitching despite herself. "It's not funny, Lance. What would your parents say?"

He shrugged. "I couldn't care less what they say. My only real family is Alex and old Karim, and I can assure you that they'll not only approve, they'll applaud the match." Then, as her face remained troubled, he sighed resignedly. "If it will make you feel any better, once my parents realize that they have to accept it, I'm sure they'll move to put a good face on it. They'll probably even try to change your name." He raised a teasing eyebrow. "How would you like to be Princess Honorina?"

"That's even worse than the other," Honey said gloomily. "You wouldn't let them do that to me, Lance."

He shook his head. "I'll let you be anything you want to be, as long as it's with me," he said softly. "I can't bear being without you, Honey. This last week has been

264

hell on earth."

"For me, too," Honey said huskily, looking up at him, her violet eyes swimming with tears. "Are you sure you won't regret this, Lance? I don't want you to make any sacrifices for my sake."

"You're the one who will be making the sacrifices," he said soberly. "As my wife, you'll have to give up your profession, for starters. It places you in much too vulnerable a position." His lips curved bitterly. "Assassination plots and kidnappings aren't all that unusual in our circles."

"Are you sure you're marrying me because you love me, and not because you need a live-in bodyguard?" Honey asked teasingly.

"I'm sure," Lance said thickly. "Oh, yes, sweetheart, I'm very sure." His lips brushed hers in a kiss of infinite sweetness, which deepened until they were both breathless, their hearts thudding erratically. "God, it's been so long since I held you like this. Do we have to talk anymore, love? I want to feel you hot around me."

She wanted that too, she thought breathlessly as his arms slid around her, his hands cupping the swell of her buttocks and bringing her urgently close to his own thrusting arousal. "Lance," she whispered lovingly, "I want —" She broke off as she felt the floor suddenly shake and vibrate beneath her feet. "Oh, my God, Lance. It's an earthquake!"

"What?" He looked down at her pale, frightened face, for a moment not comprehending anything but the hot need that was flooding him. "No, love. Much as I'd like to claim that my sexual prowess could make the earth shake for you, that is not an earthquake. We're on board Alex's yacht, and if I'm not mistaken, they've just started the engines."

He started to pull her back into his arms, but she put her hands on his chest, resisting him. "What are we doing on Alex's yacht?" She looked up at him indignantly. "You drugged me!"

"I did not," Lance denied. "I didn't know anything about it until they carried you aboard. I almost murdered Sax before Alex pulled me off him. All I told Alex was that I wanted you found and brought here." His lips tightened grimly. "He wasn't at all pleased either."

"That makes three of us," Honey said tartly. She gazed ruefully around the exotically decorated room. "I should have known as soon as I opened my eyes who was responsible for this." Then her eyes widened in alarm as she looked down at her chiffon-draped body. "And who put me into this harem outfit?"

Lance's eyes narrowed to smoldering intensity. "Would I have let my men touch you, when I meant you for myself?" he hissed melodramatically.

"Oh, Lord, where are you getting those hokey lines?" Honey groaned.

"*The Sheik,* by E. M. Hull," Lance rattled off promptly. "I thought I'd do a little in-depth research to make it more authentic. I wanted a fitting swan song to my career as Lusty Lance." He smiled with gentle raillery. "Now that I'm marrying such an earnest young woman, I'll have to concentrate on being equally sober and industrious."

Honey shook her head in amusement. Lance sober? Never in a million years. He'd always be her wild, lovable Scaramouche, even if he lived to be as old as Methuselah.

"You didn't answer me," Honey persisted. "Why are we on Alex's yacht? Is Alex on board, too?"

Lance nodded. "Because Alex's captain is going to marry us once we get on the high seas," he explained calmly. "I'm not letting you out of my sight again until we're married. We'll have a more formal ceremony once we reach Sedikhan."

"Just like that?" Honey said, snapping her

fingers. "What if I don't want to be married right here and now?"

For a moment his face was clouded with concern and there was a touch of uncertainty in his eyes. "You don't want to marry me now?"

"I didn't say that," Honey said softly. "I can't marry you fast enough to suit me. I just think it would be nice if you'd ask me instead of commanding me, Your Highness."

He took her hands in his, lifted them to his lips, and kissed the palms lingeringly, one after the other. "Will you marry me and be my love forever, Honey sweet?" he asked huskily, his expression grave and tender.

"Oh, yes," she whispered.

"Good," he said with satisfaction, his arms sliding around her. "Now that we've got that out of the way, let's get on with my seduction of your voluptuous person. Where were we?"

"You were quoting those campy lines from *The Sheik* to me," Honey said, making a face.

"Ahhh, yes," Lance said, his sapphire eyes flickering with mischief. "I have one more, which I saved for the *pièce de résistance.*"

"You do?" Honey asked warily.

He nodded, his face alight with love and the deviltry that was so much a part of him.

" 'Must I be valet as well as lover?' " he quoted softly.

And her joyous laughter was smothered against his lips.

ABOUT THE AUTHOR

Iris Johansen has more than twenty-seven million copies of her books in print, and is the *New York Times* bestselling author of *Stalemate, Killer Dreams, On the Run, Countdown, Blind Alley, Firestorm, Fatal Tide, Dead Aim,* and more. She lives near Atlanta, Georgia.